CATHY'S RING

If found call (650)266·8263

Stewart | Weisman | Brigg

RP|TEENS
PHILADELPHIA · LONDON

CATHY'S RING

If found call (650) 266-8263

Stewart | Weisman | Brigg

RP|TEENS
PHILADELPHIA · LONDON

Library of Congress Control Number: 2008933263
ISBN: 978-0-7624-3530-2
Cover design by: Ryan Hayes
Interior design by: Cathy Brigg

Running Press Book Publishers
2300 Chestnut Street
Philadelphia, PA 19103-4371

Visit Us on the web!
www.runningpress.com.

Pot of Poison (Hour of My Evil Twin)

Mom was at the hospital working the graveyard shift, and I was alone in the sweltering house. I turned off the air-conditioning as soon as she left for work, trying to save money. On hot nights like this, going to bed felt like I was pitching a tent in a toaster oven. But, in view of my spectacular failure to pay my share of the mortgage, it seemed like the least I could do. Summer was getting on, and it had been months since the dust had tasted rain. Wildfire season had started: a twenty thousand acre blaze in the Sierra foothills, and closer to home big grass fires were burning near Gilroy and Vacaville and Palo Alto. Dozens of smaller fires had left patches of blackened grass along the freeways all the way into San Francisco.

I changed into my lightest PJs, but after a second I decided not to take off the good luck charm my boyfriend, Victor, had given me—a Chinese coin threaded on a slim silver chain. He said he'd picked it up at the hospital gift shop earlier in the day. The unfamiliar weight swung and bumped against my collar bone as I trudged into the bathroom to splash my face with cold water. The eyes looking back at me from the mirror were bloodshot and exhausted. I shambled back into my bedroom and opened the window wide. There was no breeze, just the smell of burning, as if someone in the distance was holding a match to the darkness and waiting for it to catch.

I shoved the blankets off my bed and lay down on top of the sheets to wait for sleep. It had only been ten hours since I'd seen a man shot. Every time I closed my eyes I saw him looking at his bloody chest in surprise: the red blood soaking into the carpet and spattered on the wallpaper behind him. In the darkness the scorched air smelled like gunpowder.

The dead man's name was Tsao. The last thing he said before he died was, "Cathy, I will love you *forever*."

They say love warms the soul, but it burns it sometimes, too.

It was after midnight when I gave up trying to sleep. I crawled out of bed, turned on the bedroom light and closed my window. I dug a perfume bottle out of my purse and sat on the end of my bed to examine it. The bottle was almost round, shaped like a piece of crystal fruit, an apple or a peach. The heavy stopper had been fashioned into a stem with one leaf still clinging to it. The liquid inside was the color of sunlight with a teaspoon of blood mixed in.

I brought the bottle of perfume up close to my face and took out the stopper. I used to smell things by leaning in and sorta sucking air through my nose, like most people do, but when I was being trained as a perfume demonstrator at the mall they told me you actually get more fragrance if you breathe normally with your mouth a little open and waft the air toward you with your hand. I let the scent curl around me, a sweet odor like peaches with an ugly little undertone of formaldehyde and smoke. It smelled like desire without hope. Like angels burning.

My phone rang, and I picked it up instantly, thinking it would be someone in trouble, Emma or Victor. I was half right.

"You stole my perfume," said an angry voice with a sharp Texas twang.

"Hey, it's my Evil Twin, Jewel." The last time we were in a room together, ten hours ago, she was the one who killed Tsao. Then she took the money out of his wallet and forced me to give her my driver's license at gunpoint. I had been hoping I would never hear from her again. This is known as wishful thinking. "Gee, it's great to hear your voice," I said. In the background I could hear drunk people talking, bottles clinking, and the steady thud-thud of loud obnoxious dance music. "Where are you calling from?"

"Payphone at the Baptist church," Jewel said. "Listen, you took that perfume out of my purse this afternoon."

"No way," I said, turning the crystal bottle in my hands. "That would be stealing." Strictly speaking, the liquid in the bottle wasn't really perfume, it was a very special sort of poison—a complex chemical agent that took away the gift of immortality. My life had suffered a sudden and surprising

2.

infestation of immortals—my father, my boyfriend, and my boyfriend's angry ex-boss, Ancestor Lu, to name but a few—so to tell you the truth, there was something very comforting about holding that little pot of poison. In a small, mean way it felt good to think that with one well-timed spritz those godlike beings with eternal lives, lightning reflexes, and supernatural healing abilities could be reduced to ordinary human status again, at the mercy of pain and time and death like the rest of us. "Maybe you just forgot where you put it," I said. "For example, I can't find my driver's license."

"Very funny." I could hear Jewel stop to take a drink of something. "Have the cops showed up yet?"

"Not yet." Ever since I got home I had been wondering if I was about to get a visit from the Flat Feet of the Law. Because of an incident a few months back, the police had my fingerprints on file. If they got a good print from the hotel room, it was only a matter of time until their computers would identify me as a person of interest in Tsao's murder. Technically speaking I was innocent, but lying to the police is always dangerous, and telling them the truth—that my boyfriend's immortal father had a crush on me but was shot to death by my evil twin after having been dosed with a secret mortality serum—that was obviously a non-starter.

Jewel turned her mouth away from the phone. "Barkeep," she said. "Hey, Numb Nuts—yeah, you. Gimme another beer. Okay, I'm back. No cops, huh? Well, that might be good, or it might be bad." She chugged thoughtfully on her beer. "Good version, maybe you just didn't leave a lot of prints."

"What's the bad version?"

"Well, Tsao told me Ancestor Lu has some real spooky computer guys who can make things like police records just disappear. They might have wiped out your old fingerprint files."

"Why would Ancestor Lu do me a favor?"

"He wouldn't," Jewel said dryly. "The bad version is that Lu wants to take you out himself, and you're easier to whack if you aren't locked up in a nice secure jail cell."

I swallowed. "Ah."

JEWEL

"How's Denny?" Jewel asked. "Did you get him to a doctor?" Denny was Jewel's brother. Tsao had broken his arm earlier in the day. The last thing Jewel said before she killed Tsao was, "Nobody hits my brother but me."

"He's in the hospital. I was there until a couple of hours ago. He won't be playing the piano anytime soon, but he'll live."

"Listen, Cathy, you got to get him to head back to Texas. If he don't get back, the you-know-what's gonna hit the fan with his probation officer."

"Loyalty's a big thing with your brother, Jewel. He's not going to leave you here."

"I know it. That's why you're going to tell him you talked to me and I was already back home." Rap music pounded and thumped from Jewel's end of the phone.

"So, you're calling from a church," I said.

"He can tell when I'm lying but he's sweet on you. He doesn't know any better."

"Jewel—"

"*Hey*," she said sharply. "You drug my brother into this mess, Cathy. You get him out. Do it first thing tomorrow," she added. "I want to make sure he gets the message before Ancestor Lu's people take you out." Then she hung up.

It took me quite a while to get to sleep.

Scissors (Hour of Someone Coming to Kill Me)

I woke up with a gasp, terrified, staring into the darkness of my bedroom. My heart was pounding and I was listening for something, awake and electric, as if my whole skin was waiting for a sound. The clock on my bedside table said 4:13 AM.

There!

I heard it again, something gnawing at my bedroom window. Someone was working around the frame with pliers or a screwdriver. Trying to get in. Someone was coming for me, just like Jewel had said they would.

I needed help. I was alone in the darkness, and nobody would hear me scream. Ever since my dad "died" there had only been two of us in the house, my mom and me, and my mom was at the hospital working the graveyard shift. My cell phone was still lying on the dresser where I left it after Jewel hung up on me. If I grabbed it and called 9-1-1 I figured the cops would show up in time to find my dead body. If everything went well, they'd even catch my killer and put him in jail, where he would come to see the error of his ways and take up crosswords or knitting, and be featured years later in a documentary about cons who had rediscovered their humanity in prison, and finally be released on parole and start a modestly successful store selling fashionable knitwear with a jailhouse swagger—but that would be cold comfort to me, wouldn't it? Because I'd be dead. I would be dead and my mom would come out to the cemetery every six months and stare bitterly at two graves instead of one.

Scritch, scratch. Scritch-scritch, scratch. The soft complaining creak of the metal window frame being quietly pried open. Then:

- soft thumping footsteps outside, someone running up, *and*
- muffled sounds of a struggle, *and*
- the damp smack of something hard clubbing into flesh
- a gasp, *and*
- people grappling outside my window in murderous silence, *and*
- a *snap* of bone breaking
- the faint ring and slash of metal, *and*
- a *spatter*, like raindrops hitting my window.

I threw myself out of bed and scrambled across the floor on my hands and knees, waiting for the window behind me to explode in a fountain of glass—waiting for bullet holes to open in my back. I scuttled around the corner into the hallway.

- A heavy grunting *thump, and*
- bodies thudding into the side of the house.

Once out of the line of fire from the bedroom window, I got to my feet, a clumsy low crouch. I started to slap on the hallway light switch but stopped because turning on the light would just make me easier to shoot. The fact that I knew the house in the dark was the only edge I had over whoever was trying to get in.

I ran to the bathroom and yanked open the makeup drawer, pawing through it in the dark: combs, my mother's hairbrush, hair ties, compact, lipsticks, and eyebrow pencils rattling around—crap I never wore anymore. Finally my hand found the little pair of scissors my mom used to use to trim my dad's eyebrows. I shut the bathroom door, locked it, and crept into the bathtub, quietly, quietly. I pulled the shower curtain closed, steel rings whispering and clinking along the rail as I crouched with my back under the shower head. I imagined a killer forcing the door—I would have to stab down with the scissors as hard as I could because I would only get one chance.

I stood there in the bathtub, my whole body shaking with fear, the little scissors like a toy in my hand. Waiting behind the locked door like Anne Frank in her attic, wondering if I was going to die.

Another thump, hard against the side of the house. A short bubbling shriek.

Silence.

Silence.

What the *hell* was going on out there?

Waiting.

Waiting.

Waiting, barely breathing, *no sound, no sound* except my heart banging in my chest.

*

I stayed in the shower for what felt like forever, listening and listening, but after that last shriek there was nothing to hear. Finally, still clutching my scissors, I got out of the shower. I crept into the kitchen and let myself out the back door. Outside it was not yet dawn, but the night sky had begun to

6.

fade, the blackness thinning from oil paint to watercolor. The air had finally started to cool, but it still tasted like ashes in my mouth. I could hear the thin endless snarl of traffic from the freeway a couple of blocks away. With a stuttering hiss the Johnson's sprinklers came on next door. 5:00 AM.

No sounds of struggle anymore. No sound of anyone trying to get into my room.

I edged to the corner of the house and peeked around. The huddled shapes of three bodies lay on the ground outside my window. They were quite still, limbs stiff and awkwardly placed, like dolls suddenly dropped by kids called home for dinner. They were all dead—obviously dead. In a couple of places I could see pale blurs of exposed bone. I turned away and threw up.

Somewhere in the darkness a mockingbird started to sing. Dawn was coming.

Reset

Okay, I know: gruesome. Sorry about that. All I can say is, imagine how I felt.

For those of you—like me—whose attention tends to wander in class, I better stop for a quick refresher on how a perfectly ordinary girl whose worst problems were usually somewhere between Troubled Hair and Sarcastic Co-Workers came to be finding dead bodies underneath her bedroom window.

My best friend, Emma, says that different people process information in different ways, so I have prepared this Handy Chart:

All caught up? Good. We now return you to your regularly scheduled

7.

The Story So Far

Victor Chan is handsome, wealthy, charming, the perfect boyfriend... right up until he dumps me. I start ~~snooping~~ investigating.

Ancestor Lu is immortal. He wants Victor to find a way to make other people immortal, too.
   He does this by threatening to kill me.
Am I the only one that sees the irony here?

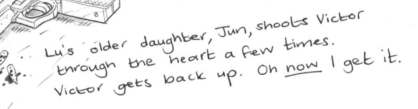

Lu's older daughter, Jun, shoots Victor through the heart a few times. Victor gets back up. Oh <u>now</u> I get it.

Victor's dad, Tsao Kuo Chiu, is another immortal. Supposedly fated to fall in love with the girl born on the first day of the first year of the Fire Tiger.
   Guess who that is?

8.

I meet Jewel on a bus. She's not immortal. She steals my stuff.

Instead of finding the secret to Eternal Youth, Victor discovers the Mouth Freshener of Death, a serum that flicks the Immortality Switch to OFF. Sometimes you just can't win for losing.

It was terrible finding my Dad dead of a heart attack. Discovering he was an immortal and had faked the whole thing pretty much sucked, too.

Jewel is hanging around with Tsao, taking advantage of her passing resemblance to yours truly. Then Tsao decides that Jewel will be more useful dead than alive. So she sprays him with the Death Serum (spritz!) and then shoots him with a .38mm (blam!)

Now I have the serum, Ancestor Lu is pissed and sending professional hitmen after me, only someone whacked instead and I have NO IDEA WHO.

Confused?

Join the Club.

programming. When we last left our heroine, she was throwing up in her backyard after having discovered three dead bodies on her lawn . . . .

Hour of the Excessive Adrenaline

I ran back to my bedroom and grabbed my cell phone, but my hand was shaking so badly I dropped it. It clattered to the floor and the back popped open, spitting out the battery. I crouched down on the floor and put the phone back together, swearing and shaking. The flash of anger helped steady my hands, so I nursed it along. "*Bloody* phone," I snarled in my best imitation Emma voice.

A terrible thought froze my hands.

What if I wasn't the only one who'd gotten a visit tonight? "Oh, my God," I whispered. I punched the speed dial number for Emma.

One ring.

Oh God, please pick up.

Two rings.

Pick up the phone, Emma. I will be a better person if you just answer the phone. I squeezed my eyes shut against a sudden image of Emma motionless in her bedroom, blood leaking from the side of her mouth and red bullet holes like ugly flowers in the middle of the Hello Kitty T-shirt she wore to bed.

Three rings.

Please just answer the phone and I will never say another mean thing as long as I—

"Hullo?" croaked a familiar British voice, blurred with sleep.

"It's about damn time you answered the phone," I hissed. "What have you got, sleeping sickness?"

"Eh? Cathy? Izzat you?"

"You have to get out of your apartment *right now*. Someone came to kill me tonight."

"Kill—" There was a sharp gasp, followed by a sudden squeak and a

10.

heavy thump.

"*EMMA!*" I screamed. I could hear sounds of a struggle, bumping and swearing, then a man's voice and a noise like a shot in my ear as someone kicked the phone. "*EMMA! ARE YOU ALL RIGHT?*"

"Peachy, thanks," Emma snarled. I could have cried with relief. "I just fell out of the bloody hammock."

I blinked. Hammock?

"Good Lord, Cathy. It's five o'clock in the morning."

So that hadn't been sounds of a struggle, exactly. That had been the sound of Emma getting pitched out of a hammock in the darkness of an unfamiliar . . . boat? And the man's voice . . . "Emma, are you staying with Pete? Were you *sleeping* with Pete?"

"Cathy!"

"Emma!"

"I was *sleeping,* not . . . *sleeping with,*" she sputtered. "Look, Pete called me last night to say there were some suspicious people lurking around my apartment. I decided it would be safer to be on the boat."

"Tell Pete he is a god," I said. "Tell him I will worship him with the fatted sheep, and the incense, and the gift certificates, for he is holy in my eyes and deserving of praise."

Emma's voice got hollow as she turned away from the phone. "Cathy says you're an idiot and could you please get a bloody light on in this cabin."

"I LOVE YOU, PETE!" I yelled. "YOU ARE A GOLDEN GOD!"

"Also she wants you to make me hot chocolate," Emma said. She turned back to the phone. "What do you mean, someone came to kill you?"

I filled her in as fast as I could. Even over the phone I could practically hear the Emma brain begin to bubble. "Thank God you're okay, Cathy! Wow. Who do you suppose got to the bad guys?"

"Victor, I guess."

"Then left you with the washing up. How very male of him."

I paced into the kitchen. Glancing out the window I could see the first pale band of daylight in the east. The bodies beside the house would be getting more visible with every passing minute.

"Cathy, have you called the police?"

"What would I tell them? That I pissed off a two-thousand-year-old man named Ancestor Lu who sent some Rent-A-Ninjas to knock me off, only they got whacked by my immortal boyfriend before he fled the scene?"

"Ah. I see the problem. Ooh, my hot chocolate," she added. "Ta."

"I'll call Victor and tell him to get his butt back here and help me clean up. In the meantime . . ." I trailed off. In the meantime… what? Emma's prize for being my one true and constant friend was that she was now directly in Ancestor Lu's line of fire, and I had no way to protect her.

"Oh, God," Emma said suddenly. "I should call my dad."

"You can tell him you spent the night at my place, if you don't want him to know about Pete."

"I'm not worried about getting in trouble, Cathy. I just need to know he's okay."

With a sudden sick lurch I imagined Mr. Cheung waking up to find a gun barrel between his teeth. For that matter, what if there were three more of these guys sitting in the parking garage at the hospital where my mom worked, waiting for her shift to end?

As long as I was around, everybody I loved was in danger.

"Okay," I said, trying to think. "Thank God Pete called you last night. You check on your dad. Tell me if—" The words caught in my throat. "Emma, I am so sorry."

"Don't panic, Cathy. We don't have time. I have to go now."

"Bye," I said, but the line was already dead.

Emma being stalked by killers. Denny lying in the hospital with his shattered arm. Tsao leaking blood into the expensive carpet of his luxury hotel. . . . I wasn't a person anymore, I was a disaster, a grass fire; everything I touched turned black and burned.

Bad Hair

I went into the bathroom and stared at myself in the mirror. My hair looked like my heart felt. I considered putting it in a ponytail. I considered shaving it all off.

Cathy, you're stalling. You have to do something about the bodies.

I parted my hair on one side, put in a barrette and went into the backyard and peeked around the side of the house. The bodies were still there. I went back to the bathroom and took out the barrette and called Victor instead. Despite the ridiculously early hour he answered on the first ring, voice sharp, as if he were expecting the call. "Cathy? What's wrong?"

"You don't know?" Victor made that kind of silence people make at me a lot, the one where they're counting to ten before saying something they're going to regret later. "Someone killed three people under my bedroom window about an hour ago. I thought it was you."

"What!"

"I don't know what I'm supposed to do with the bodies. I only have recycling bins for paper and plastic." My voice was starting to sound hysterical even to me.

"Don't move," Victor said sharply. "I'm coming over."

"It wasn't you?"

I could hear him moving swiftly through his apartment, the rustle as he grabbed his leather coat; a jingle of car keys. "Thirty minutes ago I was sitting in front of my computer trying to figure out how Ancestor Lu made all my money disappear."

"Oh." I remembered what Jewel said about Ancestor Lu having some scary-good computer spooks working for him. Apparently they could make more than just fingerprints disappear.

"Cathy, have you called the cops?"

"No."

"Good." I heard the creak of Victor's front door opening and the bang of his feet going down the porch steps.

"Victor, you're sure you didn't kill anybody?"

His feet crunched quickly down the gravel path in front of his house. "Not yet." He hung up, leaving me alone in an empty house with three bodies in the side yard and nothing to do but wait.

I tried parting my hair on the other side, but it didn't help.

Mirror, Mirror

I went back into my bedroom and put on some clothes, trying not to look at my window. I sat staring at my hair in my dresser mirror. I hadn't washed it in a while and my bangs lay limp and discouraged. I thought about grabbing a shower while I waited for Victor to show up but I figured I'd have to move the bodies and I would want to get clean after that. I was ashamed of how badly I wanted Victor just to fix everything. I wondered if that would ever change. Although he still looked like a man in his early twenties, Victor had lived more than a century. No matter how old and wise and mature I got, I was still going to be a baby compared to him. The only value I would get out of my birthdays was a few more wrinkles every year.

I picked the bottle of perfume back off the dresser. It rested in my hand like the poisoned apple the Evil Queen gives to Snow White. "Mirror, mirror, on the wall," I murmured, looking at my reflection. I have always been fascinated by how faces age, and from long practice I could see in my own features where the years were going to catch up with me: the crow's feet that would crinkle out from the corners of my eyes, the monkey-mouth lines that would form in my forties, the little widow's peak that would become more obvious as my hairline slowly crept back.

Of all the crappy jobs I had failed at, Perfume Sales Assistant was the one I was most glad to quit. Of course, I didn't *mean* to squirt the Deputy Mayor in the eye, but I can't say I was sad when they canned me afterwards. I didn't mind the teenage girls who came in to the makeup counter at the mall and tried to scam us by using our demonstrators to do their faces, except for the ones who got mouthy when I caught them shoplifting. The

14.

customers that got to me were the women my mother's age—grim or determined or desperate—still looking for husbands or trying to keep the ones they had. We sold them lipsticks and lotions, body wash and moisturizers and wrinkle-creams, but what we were really selling was one big lie, because what men want to look at is twenty-year-old girls, and you can't put that in a bottle.

My mother was thirty-eight when her husband walked out on her. The sad truth is, you don't have to be married to an immortal to have that happen to you. In twenty years Victor would still have a body you could put in an underwear ad; I would be the BEFORE picture for a plastic surgeon's Web site. My hips would be thicker and my breasts would no longer be perky and no amount of moisturizer would make my hands as smooth as they were today.

If my mother couldn't keep my dad, why did I think Victor would stick around for me? My father had said that to me, pretty much that bluntly. Was I really so much more special than her? So much more radiant and delightful than all those other women whose ordinary human husbands left them for a newer model?

I haven't written much about sex here. It's embarrassing. But for me, so much of desire is feeling desired. The other person's need is the match that lights the fuse. But it seemed as if desire was one of the things you let go of when you were immortal. Tsao said, *my blood turned to ashes for a thousand years.* In fact, thinking back, it was only after Jewel dosed him with the mortality serum that he started to lose his temper, to feel the sharp knife of emotion peel back his skin and leave him raw again.

What if my feelings for Victor—not the friendship, but the other part, the tingling, electric, dangerous part—turned out to be just a little grass fire after all? A flame that would burn itself out in a year or two, leaving him restless and bored. Leaving me waiting for his desire like a candle waiting for a match that would never strike?

Honestly, wasn't that the way it would go? Right now, today, he might say he would love me forever. He might even believe we would be together

15.

for a thousand years, but the hard truth was that I would spend nine hundred and thirty of them in an ashtray on his mantelpiece.

Maybe that's part of why I hadn't told Victor I had the mortality serum. He would always be a handsome prince, but my princess days were burning away one birthday candle at a time. I picked up the little perfume bottle and tucked it back into my purse. Every woman knows that sooner or later the mirror will tell her she is no longer the fairest in the land. When that day comes, a piece of poisoned fruit is a handy thing to have around.

Victor Arrives (Hour of the Eternal Boyfriend)

"That took a while," I said when Victor finally came through the front door. I was trying not to sound accusing but I didn't quite make it.

He cupped my face in his hands. "You okay?"

My skin prickled, flushing from where his hands were touching me. So unfair. I pulled back. "No, not okay," I said. "Not even slightly."

I led him to the narrow strip of yard beside the house, between my window and the fence that separated our yard from the O'Malley's. It was broad daylight now, and the muted hum of traffic from the freeway a couple of blocks away was picking up. From the street the bodies had mostly been hidden by our A/C unit, but if you looked hard you could see a couple of legs poking out and the pale blur of one face, so I had taken the wheelbarrow out of the garage and put it in the front yard to screen off the area.

Victor stepped around the air conditioner and crouched beside the corpses. There were two men and a woman. The first man was a white guy in his twenties, crew-cut, ex-military to judge by the globe-and-anchor Marine tattoo on his forearm. He had a broken neck. The second man was Latino, mid-forties, pock-faced, hard-muscled. The woman was Chinese, mid-thirties, stocky build. There was a gun in her hand with a silencer screwed onto the barrel. The fingers on that hand were broken.

Victor patted all three of them down, taking a gun from each of them and combat knives from the two men. He looked brisk and efficient, and I

16

wondered how many times he had done this before. I could feel a kind of glassy distance between the dead people and my heart: *I will not care about these things. I will not be here. I will not feel this.*

Victor reached delicately under the collar of the dead woman's shirt and pulled out a loop of silk cord. A Chinese coin dangled from the end of it, glinting in the early morning light.

"Hey, that's just like the one you gave me in the hospital yesterday!" I squinted. "You said it was a good luck charm."

It was Victor's turn to look uncomfortable. "Mmm."

I reached inside my shirt and pulled out the necklace. The coin was identical. "You didn't buy this at the hospital gift shop, did you?"

"Not exactly."

I looked at the dead bodies, and then my hands flew behind my neck, fumbling to undo the chain, feeling suddenly as if I was wearing a necklace of spiders. "Oh, *gross.*" I threw the chain and coin down on the grass, revolted. "What *is* it?"

Victor sighed. "Lucky Joy Cleaners. Company badge."

"A *cleaning* company?"

Victor settled back on his haunches, studying the two matching coins. He picked one up and held it, a bronze disk between his brown fingers. "Not that kind of cleaner."

"Oh." It slowly dawned on me what he meant. "I see."

Victor tucked the necklaces into a pocket. "I caught one of their operatives at the hospital yesterday, a guy I recognized from Ancestor Lu's place. I went down and, uh, convinced him to go away," he said. "That's where your necklace came from."

"Why would you give me that thing?"

"You looked like you could use a present," he said. "Besides, I figured if they found you and saw the badge, they might hesitate to do anything, or at least waste some time calling back to headquarters for instructions." He ran his eyes over the dead bodies. "Normally these guys are very good at what they do. You should be lying on the bottom of the bay in a plastic bag by now . . . ."

17.

"Except somebody else got to them first."

Victor picked up the silenced gun, popped a lever, and a magazine slid out of the grip. He counted the bullets. "No shots fired. Whoever did this to them did it fast."

"Like an immortal."

"Either that or a cop with super speed," he agreed. "Jun, maybe?"

My mind reeled. Jun was Ancestor Lu's daughter. The last time we met she had almost killed me, although in all fairness it hadn't been personal. The person she wanted to kill was Little Sister, Ancestor Lu's ten-year-old human daughter. Jun thought Lu's love for his kid was driving him to do all sorts of irrational things, so with typical immortal logic, she figured she might as well nip the problem in the bud by doing away with the kid. All very rational and yet psychotic, which I was beginning to think was an immortal trademark. "I suppose she is sort of technically on our side, but as much as she hates what her dad is doing, I can't see her doing late night bodyguard duty for me."

"I asked her to keep an eye on you," Victor said. This time he wasn't looking at me.

Some prankster had apparently pulled the fire alarm in the cafeteria of my heart, because suddenly it got very loud and hard to think. "You've been talking to Jun?"

"She opposes her father. She thinks his use of the mortality serum is criminal and wrong and brings shame on her family," Victor said. "And frankly, I figured we could use all the help we could get."

"We? Who is this 'we'?" I asked. "Am I part of the 'we' that decided to get Jun involved, because I don't remember that."

Victor moved over to the two men and removed the Lucky Joy Cleaners coins from around their necks. "Cathy, we aren't married, and you don't sign my paycheck. I'm not going to send you a memo about every conversation I have when you aren't around." He pocketed the remaining coins. "I would think this," he said, jerking his head at the bodies, "would be proof enough that we could use Jun's help. What do you have against her, anyway?"

She's beautiful, she's immortal, she is obviously and screamingly a better choice to be your girlfriend than I am. "She has perfect hair," I muttered. Victor looked at me incredulously.

Guys are so dumb.

The Wheelbarrow

We used the wheelbarrow to move the dead people into our garage. It was hard to get the bodies balanced and the wheelbarrow kept tipping over.

I don't want to write about that.

Time Off For Bad Behavior

Victor asked me for some plastic bags and a bottle of bleach and told me to wait in the house while he loaded the bodies into his car. Fifteen minutes later he knocked softly on the kitchen door.

"Almost done." Our eyes met. For an immortal man with infinite healing powers, he looked awfully tired. "You should change. Get out of those clothes," he said. "Moving the bodies, there's probably evidence on them."

Evidence meaning skin cells or clothing fibers or strands of blood-spattered hair.

"Okay," I said.

I asked Victor to give me a ride to the hospital because I wanted to check in on my mom. This wasn't quite true, but then again, he hadn't exactly been George Washington about the Chinese coin necklace, so I figured it all evened out. The truth was I needed to disappear. It seemed clear to me now that everyone I loved would be in danger as long as I was around. But I didn't have the money for a plane ticket, and I couldn't just steal my mother's car and light out for the territories. That's where Denny came in. Jewel was completely right when she blamed me for getting her brother mixed up in my life. I figured the least I could do was get him back to Texas where he would be safe, or at least as safe as you can be in a state where the climate is like the surface of mercury and salad is something you eat in Jell-O.

The right thing to do would be to get Denny on a highway headed out of state as fast as possible. I would hitch a ride with him partway to Texas and then disappear one night while he was asleep so neither he, Jewel, nor any of my friends and family ever heard of me again.

The Other Man

It was 6:40 a.m. by the time Victor dropped me off at the hospital. Not quite visiting hours, but the nurses knew me and I scored some serious Daughter Points by telling them I had stopped by to pick up my mom when her shift ended at seven. They told me what a great kid I was and how much they wished their daughters were like me.

If they only knew.

In the meantime, I had twenty minutes to sneak up to see Denny; twenty minutes to lay the groundwork for my disappearance. When I poked my nose into his room he was standing at the window in a blue paper hospital gown that showed off his hairy calves. At 5'8" and 215 pounds, squat, square, bruised, and battered, Denny looked as if he had been abandoned in a junkyard as a baby and raised by wild refrigerators. He had a long white cast on his left arm that went from his wrist to the tattoo just under his bicep. The tattoo said Die Trying, and if he stuck around me much longer, he might do just that.

"When fashion designers go to hell," I said, "all the runway models look just like you."

Denny turned around. His bruised face was spectacular, puffy and mottled like a bunch of bananas a week past their Best Before date. A crumpled grin dented his swollen face. "*Ow*, god dammit! Don't make me laugh."

"You still mean to head home tomorrow?"

"Depends on how fast you get out of this room. Every time I'm around you any length of time someone shows up to beat the crap out of me."

20.

I winced. Victor had pasted him pretty thoroughly two days before, but it was Tsao who'd broken his wrist and elbow yesterday, when the two of us had bungled into a memorial services which had been strictly No Mortals Allowed. "If it makes you feel any better, the guy who broke your arm is dead."

"Yeah. Emma and them told me." Denny looked away, jaw working. "Jewel did him?"

"It was self-defense, Denny."

"That's gonna change her. Killing a man." Denny closed his eyes. He looked tired. "That's a thing you don't come back from."

"It was self-defense, I swear it. It wasn't Jewel being . . ."

"Jewel," he said drily.

"He was going to push her off the balcony on the thirteenth floor." I grabbed his good hand and squeezed it, as if the truth of that was something he could feel through the skin. "Believe me, Denny. If Jewel hadn't pulled the trigger, I think we'd both be dead."

"Did you tell the cops that?"

"Not exactly." Denny gave me a look and I hurried on. "There's no way to explain about the immortals is there, really? I mean, if we told the police what actually happened, either we'd get cited for contempt of court or end up doing fingerpaint therapy at the California State Happy House for the Terminally Deranged."

Denny looked down to where I was still holding his one good hand, then looked back at me, concern in his bruised face. "What about you? Are you okay?"

"Me? Sure."

"I remember the first time I saw someone get shot." Denny slid his hand out from between mine, reached up and scratched his stubbled chin. "Shook me up."

"How old were you?"

"Seven? No, I tell a lie. Six, I reckon."

It hit me one more time that Denny and Jewel had lived a life I could only imagine. I took a deep breath. "Jewel called me last night. From Texas."

21.

Scientific *un*fact:.
Lying requires 38% more oxygen than telling the truth.

It was a good thing I was a noble person trying to save Denny's life, because otherwise telling such a bald-faced lie would have made me feel cheaper than used Kleenex.

Denny shot me a sharp look. "Texas? That was quick. She say where she was staying?"

"Not exactly. She was calling from a bar, though."

His swollen mouth puckered in a grimace and the suspicious look faded. "Yeah, that sounds about right."

"She wanted you to know she was home safe, and you should get back before your probation officer knows you ever left. And . . . I was hoping you would take me with you."

Denny looked at me for what felt like a long time. I knew he liked me, the way girls know, but this wasn't that kind of look. Not the Sly Checkout, the friendly I'm Available expression, or (my personal least favorite) the Studied Air of Mystery. Just a long, steady considering look.

"Usually I don't get a whole room to myself when I go to hospital," he said, shambling into the little bathroom beside his bed. "Mostly they just stitch me up in the hallway behind emergency and send me on my way. This is swanky."

"Victor's paying. Don't worry about it—he's got lots of money." Well, he used to, until Lu's cyberspooks had made it disappear, but that didn't seem like something Denny needed to know.

Jewel's brother winced at the mottled face that looked back at him out of the mirror. He picked up a disposable razor from the hospital store and tried to open the package with one hand. "Um, could you . . . ?"

"The first blade shaves them close; the second blade shaves them closer." I split the cellophane with my patented girl-type fingernails and handed him the plastic razor inside. "The third blade takes the whiskers and bundles them into little bales, while the fourth blade . . ."

"Makes them into trout flies to sell on the black market." Denny dabbed shaving cream onto his bruised face, then put down the can and spread the cream around very gingerly, just using his fingertips. "Say you did come with me. You gonna need a place to stay?" Very casual.

I imagined what it would be like to wake up in an apartment with someone who wasn't my mother; to hear coffee making in the next room and country & western music on the radio. Sausage and scrambled eggs for breakfast, maybe, and then I would grab an apron and head out for my shift at some diner with a name like the Flapjack Ranch, dropping Denny off at his auto-body job on the way. I could live like Jewel for once and not have to think about Victor or immortals or my dad. I wouldn't have to worry about making a fortune for Emma or saving the world. I could pretend I never met Ancestor Lu, my mom would get on fine without me, and Victor never loved me anyway, not really.

"A place to stay?" I said. "I dunno. I guess I hadn't thought that far ahead."

Denny picked up his razor. "Did you have a fight with Victor?"

"No! What makes you say that?"

Denny pulled the razor gently down one cheek, so a stripe of bruised skin showed through the shaving cream. "One thing about Jewel, when one guy throws her out of his trailer at daybreak, she's in some other fella's doublewide by sunset."

"I am not like Jewel!"

Denny glanced up and our eyes met in the bathroom mirror. "Un-hunh."

"This isn't about romance, this is about staying alive," I said. "Ancestor Lu sent some goons after me this morning. If I hang around here, he's just going to keep coming after me. Me and everyone I care about."

"Ah," Denny said. "Better to stick with me, then."

Ack! "I didn't mean it like that!"

"Well, sure you did." He tilted up his chin and ran the razor along his neck. I could see the bump of his pulse in a vein under his throat. The razor blade sliding over it. Tough as he was, he was still only human—all his hopes and dreams held together by nothing more than a few millimeters of skin. The handle of the razor looked thin and cheap in his thick hands. His fingers were nicked with scar lines, grimy rings of motor oil still under his fingernails. "I know what you meant. Sometimes it seems like everything you touch turns to crap."

23.

Hamburger Girl

for writing orders on back of head.

for wiping up coffee, pecan pie, or little Bubba's spit-up

Cathy Sue

"Yeah."

Denny tapped the razor on the edge of the sink to get the extra shaving cream off. Little gobs of it slid slowly down the side of the sink, flecked with bits of stubble. "You want to bring Emma along?"

"No. Absolutely not. You have to promise not to tell anyone—not Emma or Pete or my mom."

"Or Victor." He looked at me in the mirror again.

"Or Victor," I said.

"It's not like I think I'm all that," Denny said. He rinsed off the disposable razor and then dropped it in the blue plastic garbage pail under the bathroom sink. He met my eyes. "But I don't intend to be anybody's consolation prize."

Intensive Care (Hour of Looking After My Mother)

Denny said he was aiming to get discharged first thing tomorrow morning. That gave me just about twenty-four hours to put my affairs in order before his Mustang showed up at my front door. We shook on the deal, and then I hurried out of the room to get a ride home with my mom.

I caught up with her just as she was signing out at the nursing station in intensive care. She looked tired and there were a couple of fresh stains on her scrubs, dull red and brown. You have to be pretty tough to work a shift in the ICU. Doris, her shift partner, saw me first and flicked her eyes in my general direction. Mom turned around. "Cathy! What are you doing here? Are you sick?"

"I'm fine. I was in the neighborhood, so—"

"At seven o'clock in the morning?" My mother put her hand on my forehead to check for a fever.

Right. Not very in character. "I was out late."

Her eyes narrowed. "The moment we get home I'm checking the bathroom garbage for a home pregnancy test wrapper."

"No good. I tossed it in the Mueller's garbage can."

25.

"Cathy—!"

"Joke! I promise I'm not pregnant."

My mother squinted at me. "You're never up at this hour."

"Hey," Doris said, "If your kid isn't stoned, pregnant, or bleeding . . ."

"Be grateful and shut up?" Mom grabbed her purse from behind the counter at the nursing station. "I guess actually knowing what goes on in your life would be too much to ask."

"Honestly, best left to the imagination." I took the gym bag with her spare change of clothes in it. "It's really more glamorous that way."

There was a closed-circuit security camera in the elevator. I had never noticed that before. "Mom? Did you see anyone unusual around last night?"

"Two kids from a fight at a bar, one with glass cuts, the other one shot and with a collapsed lung," Mom said. "One car crash—single vehicle accident, thank God—and one heart attack. The usual."

"Did you happen to see anyone wearing a necklace with a Chinese coin on it, by any chance?"

"Is Victor giving jewelry to some other girl?" My mother ruffled my hair sympathetically. "I told you that would never last, sweetheart. You should really stick to dating boys your own age."

"You know what, Mom?" Our eyes met. "That's probably really good advice."

*

Nobody murdered us in the parkade.

Lying

I went home with Mom and fed her a quick breakfast. It was the last day I would ever spend at home, but I made her eggs as if everything was perfectly normal. My mother is not a trusting woman, but she talked about chores and work and the weather as if I was going to be there. She chatted and drank her decaf coffee and never dreamed that I was going to abandon her. I just cooked and smiled and nodded my head until her breakfast was

26.

over and she shambled off to bed.

I lie a lot and I'm good at it. I used to be kind of proud of that.

"G'night, kiddo," my mother said, closing the bedroom door behind her. "See you later."

"See you," I said.

I'm not proud of it anymore.

Cashing Out (Hour of Memories for Sale)

I needed money. The sad truth was that after most of a summer spent working at a variety of unimaginably boring, entry level jobs, I didn't have enough cash in the bank to buy second-hand underwear. If I wanted money, I was going to have to sell something to get it. My laptop and my art supplies were too precious to give up, and besides that I didn't have much in this world but a selection of slightly eccentric clothes scrounged from local thrift stores and enough hair mousse to give Mohawks to a herd of bison. I did have one other asset, though: an attic full of genuine Michael Vickers art. Back when my father had been dead, I wouldn't have dreamed of selling one of his paintings. Had I known he'd merely faked his own death as a way to abandon me and my mother, I would have cheerfully stuffed each precious canvas into a vending machine in exchange for a can of pop or a bag of chips.

I was up in my dad's studio, looking through his paintings, when my cell rang. It was Emma. I pounced on the phone. "Emma! Is your dad . . . ?"

"Yeah, he's okay." Relief flooded through my body. "I told him the apartment was being fumigated and moved him to a Motel 6."

"Thank God." I cradled the phone against my ear. As always, my father's studio was haunted with memories: the smell of oil paints and turpentine, sunlight glinting off the jam jars he kept his brushes in, little tubes of colors only artists know: cobalt chromite green, cadmium yellow, quinacridone red. And of course the memory of finding my father dead on the floor, his hand stretched out, skin grey and cold. Lips tinted manganese blue.

"What are you doing?" Emma said.

27.

An assortment of my dad's paintings was stacked against the wall, some framed and finished, others still on studio canvas. I started flipping through them one by one, looking for something I could sell. "Housecleaning," I told Emma. I figured that sounded better than "stealing from the dead."

"Cleaning? You?"

"Gee, thanks." I paused at an oil painting of a snowy egret my dad had done a few months before he faked his death. Pretty good, in a Robert Bateman kind of way. I pulled it aside as one I might be able to sell. "Got any good ideas on how I can raise some cash?"

"Get a job?"

"A good plan in theory, but it doesn't seem to be working out for me."

Emma sighed. "I can probably lend you a few bucks. What do you need it for?"

Never seeing you again. "Oh, nothing in particular."

"It's paints, isn't it? I know oil paints aren't cheap, but that's where the money is," Emma said. "I've been doing some research. Honestly, Cathy, this is a capital expense. You have to be willing to invest in yourself. Find a supplier online and I'll buy you some decent quality oil paints."

"Emma, you don't have any money either!"

"We can put it on a credit card."

"You HATE debt," I said. "Unless . . . wait a sec. Exactly which credit card were you going to put that on?"

"VISA," she said brightly.

"That's not what I meant. Are you running around charging things on Tsao's card?"

"No! Absolutely not! . . . Yet. It's not like he's going to be needing the money," she said sullenly.

"Did Pete talk you into this?"

I discovered my cell phone had a whole separate channel just for delivering Incredulous Scorn. "Did *Pete* try to talk *me* into something?"

"Right. Forget I said that." If Emma ever went for a life of crime, it would be entirely her own decision and she would corner the market in

evil with a business plan and a comprehensive set of spreadsheets. "Are you staying on the *Moonshine* tonight?" The *Moonshine* was the little sailboat Pete lived on; the one with the hammock Emma had fallen out of face first to start the day.

"Yeah, I think so. Victor called Pete, actually. They're trying to figure out what Ancestor Lu's computer geeks did with Victor's money." She must have turned her face away from the phone, because her voice got muffled and distant. "How's it coming?"

Pete launched into a lengthy answer and I tuned out; Geekspeak is a foreign tongue to me, even when I'm not trying to follow it secondhand. I set aside another few paintings, sticking mostly with oils in nice frames—a pair of goldfinches, a barn owl painted mug-shot close to focus on those psychotic eyes owls have, and a red-tailed hawk, as well as an older painting of swirls and spatters from Dad's Expressionist period. There were also a couple of odd period pieces, set in the 1930s. One was a fight scene: two boxers going at it in a ring watched by a mob of people dressed in Depression-era clothes, long coats and fedoras. Of course it might not have been a period piece at all, come to think of it: my dad might have painted it in 1931 for all I knew. I slowed down, imagining him alive back then, looking just the same as he did now, wearing a wool suit and slouch hat, calling people on candlestick phones you had to dial instead of pushing buttons. No computers. No TV.

Each new age of the world must be like a stage set to the immortals, I thought: a museum diorama or fairground attraction. Nothing would look new after a while, because you would know that every up-to-date fashion or stylish haircut was just a few years from being old-fashioned, obsolete, forgotten.

I found another Depression-era painting, a cheap diner with neon lights outside and a soda fountain behind the counter, the scene captured late on a rainy night in some big city. Inside the diner, a traveling salesman with a cheap attaché case sat on a red vinyl stool, nursing a cup of coffee and a cigarette like a man who had no home to go to.

29

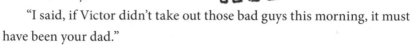

"Cathy?"

"Oh, sorry, Emma. What?"

"I said, if Victor didn't take out those bad guys this morning, it must have been your dad."

"No way." I blinked, trying to imagine my father taking on a group of hired killers. The idea was absurd. Putting a wounded bird in a shoebox and nursing it to health—yes. That was my father. Deadly assassin? Not a chance.

"You're still acting like he's just some middle-aged guy that likes to paint birds," Emma said. "He's an immortal, Cathy. You know he must have fought in wars. He was a conquistador, remember?"

It was true. I had even found some of his sketches from that time, five-hundred-year-old drawings of the plants and animals of the New World, made when he had been forced to travel with Ponce de Leon in search of the Fountain of Youth. "He wasn't a soldier, though. He was just a guide."

"Maybe that time. But any man who has been alive that long has killed people, Cathy. Victor fought in lots of wars, and your dad is hundreds of years older than him."

"No, I just think—"

"He might have crossed the Delaware with Washington," Emma said relentlessly. "Or been waiting for him in a red coat, assuming he had the sense to be on the right side," she added, in her most British accent.

Victor, when he fought, had this trick of making time run slowly, cutting down his enemies as if they were standing still. It was horrible to think of my father that way, but of course he would be able to do those things, too.

Maybe he *had* left the hired killers like dolls, broken beneath my window.

"He is an immortal, Cathy."

"So . . . human life just doesn't mean very much to him."

"I didn't say that!"

"I did."

Emma sighed. "Things will look better when you've had a little more sleep."

"Emma?"

30

"Yeah?"

Thank you, I didn't say. *If I had only known I was going to disappear I would have told you how much your friendship meant to me. I would have told you I always knew you were better than me—not just smarter but a better person, tougher and more principled. I would have told you to wear red more often and tried to make you realize how pretty you can be when you let yourself smile. But now it's too late. When you make your first million, I won't be there. I won't get to dance at your wedding or make goofy pictures for ridiculously cute Emma babies. You deserved so much more than I gave you. I always thought there would be time to make it back some day, to show you that you were anything but an extra in* The Cathy Show. *You were the main event.*

"Cathy? You still there?"

"Sorry, yeah. Still here."

"What were you going to say?"

"Nothing important." I had to hang up before she could tell I was crying. "Just . . . good-bye."

LOST

Rising Into Silence

Half an hour later Mom was asleep and I was driving around the South Bay, heading for the galleries most likely to buy my dad's paintings. I figured I'd try Grant's in Mountain View first because they paid the best. Then I would hit High Sierra Galleries in Palo Alto, and then a couple of places closer to the city. With any luck I should be able to scrounge up a few hundred bucks.

The day was turning hot again. A thin film of ash had settled on the car overnight, and the air still tasted of distant smoke. I stopped at a gas station to wipe the windows clean. Afterwards I turned on the car radio, which is what I was going to have for company instead of friends, but I didn't know any of the songs. It was funny to think that after one more day I might never talk to Emma again, never see my house, never argue with my mom. It was the right thing to do, for their safety and mine, but *never* was a hard idea

31.

to get my head around. Part of me kept wanting to believe it would only be a few weeks, a month or two of exile, but that was just wishful thinking. Ancestor Lu wasn't simply a powerful enemy, he was immortal. There would be no such thing as waiting him out.

When you're a regular human girl with strictly low-end makeup and discouraged hair, forever seems like a very long time.

I felt lonely and light-headed and a little numb. The towns I had driven around all my life seemed weirdly unfamiliar, and I got lost twice on the way to Grant's. I kept thinking they must have renamed the streets, but no doubt they were nestled between their sidewalks the same as always. It was me that had become a stranger. I felt oddly disconnected, as if I had somehow slipped out of my own life, escaping like a fairground balloon from a child's hand. Weightless and solitary, drifting up into a future as blank and empty as the sky. Rising into silence.

Contemporary Relevance
(Hour of the Orange Almond Biscotti)

Grant's Gallery had changed its name to Bernini Fine Art and Mocha Bar, and instead of Mrs. Grant minding the shop there was an espresso bar manned by a girl with a nose ring and tattoos. "We don't buy paintings," she said, looking at the stack of canvasses under my arm.

"My dad used to show here."

The counter girl looked pointedly from the graffiti-influenced propaganda posters and angsty Mark Ryden wannabes currently on the walls to the snowy egret painting at the front of my stack. "Really?"

I had a brief vision of hooking my finger through her nose ring and yanking it like a fire alarm. "Does Mrs. Grant still work here?"

"The owners have decided to move the gallery in a more contemporary direction." Nose Ring Girl turned around and organized an artfully arranged plate of biscotti where the Old Masters postcard rack had been last time I had been here with my dad. We had been talking about Franz Hals, and I remember thinking about the way the California sunlight flashed on my dad's high balding forehead; how Hals would have rendered that with a slap of white paint that looked careless up close but perfect from six feet away.

I hefted my armload of canvasses. "My dad painted these. Michael Vickers. Grant's used to sell a lot of his stuff. He . . . passed away," I stammered.

Nose Ring Girl sighed and leaned across the counter. "Listen," she said, "between you and me, I'd rather look at birds." She ran her eyes over the strident political commentary pieces hanging on the walls of Bernini's Fine Art and Mocha Bar: blobs of red and green paint, stick figures getting interrogated by military police, and activist slogans. "I go to art school with these guys and they mean it and all, but, you know, spend a little less time lecturing me on world politics and a little more time learning to draw." She rolled her eyes. "But . . . that's what the gallery sells now. And trust me, money is the only thing Maggie Grant cares about. Nowadays the big money around here is thirty-year-old guys with stock options at Google, okay, and they aren't buying pictures of cranes."

33.

"Snowy egrets."

"They aren't buying those, either." Nose Ring Girl stuck out her hand. "I'm Phoebe."

"I'm broke," I said.

"That's traditional. Want a biscotti? Orange-almond, today. On the house," she added, seeing me hesitate.

"Oh." I took the biggest one. "Thanks. My name is Cathy."

"Yeah, I remember you coming in here with your dad." I must have looked surprised. "My hair was a different color, and I didn't have any body art back then." She pointed at the snowy egret painting. "Listen, I can give you forty bucks for that."

"Forty dollars! The *paint* probably cost that much!"

"Not for the painting," Phoebe said apologetically. "For the frame."

Our eyes met.

"My dad . . . ." It was hard to remember he wasn't dead, not really. Just dead to me. "He spent a lifetime learning to . . ."

"I know." Phoebe looked at me. "But that's the life of an artist. As you know," she added. And I did, of course. Van Gogh sold one painting before he shot himself in the chest and died at the age of thirty-seven. Caravaggio died broke, sick, and in exile. *The Muse only cares about the art*, my father used to say, *she doesn't give a damn about the artist. She will squeeze you like a tube of paint, squeeze you empty if that's what it takes to get the work out of you.*

"Good frames cost money," Phoebe said gently. "Want me to take it into the back?"

It would probably take her fifteen minutes to lever the frame open and ease the canvas out. Or she could just cut the painting out with an Exacto knife and stack the frame against a wall until they had a piece they could use it for, something edgy and contemporary. Something that would sell. As for the snowy egret, well, one of us would crumple it up and pitch it in the trash can or the fireplace.

"I can't," I said. "I'm sorry."

Phoebe nodded. "Come back if you change your mind."

Maybe it was just my imagination, but I think she was relieved.

High Sierra Art & Gifts (Hour of My Father's Old Friend)

In 1967 George Purefoy, a graduate student at the London School of Economics, walked out of a class on international monetary policy, took the Underground to Heathrow Airport without bothering to stop by his flat or say good-bye to his fiancée, and purchased a one-way ticket to San Francisco to be part of the Summer of Love. He bought a guitar, dropped acid, wrote poems about love, painted psychedelic watercolors because he couldn't afford oil paints, found the guitar didn't get him girls, put down the guitar, took up mushrooms, did psychedelic drawings in Doodle Art markers because he couldn't afford watercolors, found a girl, lost the girl, wrote poems about despair, found himself desperately scrounging other people's cigarette ends and panhandling for money, took up reading Gary Snyder, got a job as a forest fire lookout in the High Sierra, converted to Buddhism, took up green tea, took up calligraphy, kept a vow of silence for almost seven months, and worked for the National Parks Service for years and years, while presidents—Nixon, Ford, Carter, Reagan—built and faded away like cloud formations over the mountains. Then, in the spring of 1989, completely oblivious to the fall of the Berlin Wall or the invention of the cell phone, he was suddenly overwhelmed by the urge to watch soccer on TV, listen to early Beatles songs, and follow the financial markets in the daily newspaper over a nice cup of coffee and a Danish every morning, just as he used to do back in the autumn of 1966 when he had been young and clever and had his whole life in front of him.

During all this time he lost not the faintest trace of his English accent.

For the last fifteen years he had been running a gallery that featured postcards with Zen koans on them, coffee mugs with Native American designs, and paintings of California landscapes and wildlife. My dad had sold quite a few pieces through the gallery. I had gone to Grant's first because they paid the best, but Mr. Purefoy had known my dad for a long

35.

time, and even if he didn't get the kinds of prices Maggie Grant did, he was my surest bet for ready cash.

The first thing I noticed about the High Sierra Gallery when I pulled up was that the sign needed repainting. The background was dingy and the California sun had faded the lettering giving it a faint feeling of neglect. The bell over the front door was broken, too; when I went inside it made only a single dull clack instead of the cheerful jingle I remembered. Mr. Purefoy didn't look up at the sound of the broken bell. He was hunched on a stool behind his counter, frowning at a coin in his hands—a quarter, or a nickel maybe. I got the feeling the gallery had come on hard times, and a sudden knot of anxiety twisted in my stomach. I needed cash and I needed it quick.

"Hey, Mr. Purefoy," I said, in the bright, cheerful voice I had used to sell Frozen Cookie Dough for the School Art Society fundraiser before the unfortunate incident with the pottery kiln that got me kicked out of the club. "Do I have something for you!"

"No, thank you," he said absently, "the gallery already sponsors the Just for Kix girls soccer club." He glanced up. "I'm sure the florist next door . . . Oh, my God. You're Mike Vickers' girl." The life drained from his face, leaving it as pale and abandoned as the faded sign outside; as if George Purefoy's portrait was something you wouldn't paint in oils, but in ink wash on newsprint.

"Cathy Vickers, large as life and twice as natural," I said, beaming the full force of my Cheerful Mind Control Rays at him. "I have some paintings here my dad was saving just for you!"

The last time I had seen Mr. Purefoy he still looked very much the dapper gallery owner, with distinguished salt-and-pepper hair, a neatly trimmed beard and animated hands. Now the hair was all white and the beard was getting straggly. In the visual arts, forgetting about appearances is not a good sign. His hands were splotched with liver spots and actually shaking so I still couldn't make out what he was holding. He turned quickly and I heard a clink as he put something down beside the cash register. "I was so sorry to hear about your father."

36.

I forced myself to keep smiling. "It was hard at first, but it's been a couple of years now, and I think we've all come to peace with it." Also I found out the bastard wasn't dead, but why dwell on details. "Unfortunately, Mom and I are a bit pressed for money," I said, doing my best Plucky Young Lass. "Dad always said that if we were ever in trouble, you were the one person we could count on."

Mr. Purefoy flinched. "It's not that . . . I know your father's work meant a lot to you . . ." Our eyes met.

"I'm not disrespecting him," I said, in case he thought it was low-class of me to be hocking my dad's stuff. "It's just, sometimes you get into a tight spot, you know? Sometimes you don't have any choices any more." That at least was the dead level truth. "My Mom is in trouble right now. I need to take care of her."

"As it happens, my mother is very sick, too." Mr. Purefoy picked up a postcard from the revolving display on the counter and fingered it absently. "You know, it's amazing to me," he remarked, putting the card carefully back into the rack, "just how much money it costs to die." I had no idea what to say to that, but thankfully I didn't have to come up with anything. "Of course, you are quite right. Sometimes there aren't any choices anymore." His whole manner became much more collected, as if he had come to a decision. "I'd be delighted to look through your father's paintings. I'm sure we can come to some sort of accommodation."

Relief flooded through me. "Thanks. Wow, you have no idea what this means to me."

His smile stayed fixed for the briefest instant, and then brightened. "Delighted I can help. Just let me step into the back room for a moment and make a quick phone call. I shan't be a minute."

He headed through a door behind the counter and I let out a huge sigh. I had brought five paintings in with me, all the wildlife stuff, leaving the Depression pieces in the car. If he bought half of them, he could probably be pretty sure of selling three of the five. He usually sold my dad's stuff in the three hundred dollar range on a sixty percent commission. Obviously

37.

I couldn't ask for the whole shot in advance, but even if Mr. Purefoy gave me a fifty percent advance on say two paintings, that would be, uh, uh.. . I found my fingers moving, as they always did when I tried to work out math problems. I leaned over the counter, wondering if Mr. Purefoy had a calculator I could borrow, and my eye fell on something glinting by the cash register. It was the coin he had been holding in his hand when I came in, but it wasn't a quarter or a nickel.

It was a Chinese coin with a hole through the middle.

The door behind the counter opened, and Mr. Purefoy came back into the gallery. "Now, let's see what you have there, shall we?"

"Who were you calling?" I asked.

"Just a business call. Let's talk about those paintings, shall we?" He pointed at the barn owl. "That's good. I'm sure I can sell that one."

"How much?"

"Oh, I don't know. Four hundred dollars?" I stayed quiet, unless you count the noise my heart was making hammering against my ribs. Mr. Purefoy frowned. "Five hundred?"

"And fifty percent commission?"

"That seems fair."

"I've got to go," I said. I started gathering up the paintings stacked against the wall. "I need to think this over."

"No!" Mr. Purefoy paused to reaffix his smile and then started to walk out from behind the counter. "I can make you a better offer. I really think you should stay."

I took off running. The broken bell clacked as I yanked the door open and sprinted to my car. My hands went spastic on me and it took me three tries to get the key into the ignition. I stomped on the gas and the car roared to life as Mr. Purefoy ran out of his shop, talking on his cell phone. The tires squealed and I peeled off down the street.

what was Jewel going to do with my drivers license?

The Messenger
(Hour of the Yellow-Rumped Warbler)

My blood was buzzing and crawling with adrenaline, as if a nest of wasps had been trapped inside my body. I gunned the car for the freeway entrance ramp and found myself heading for San Francisco at ninety miles an hour. It was all I could do to force myself to slow to traffic speed and try to calm down. Obviously Ancestor Lu's henchmen were making the rounds of all the galleries my dad used to frequent. I fiddled with the car radio until I found a station playing loud anxious emo music and blasted down 101 North to San Francisco, driving as if the highway was paved with Rent-A-Ninjas and I needed to mow them all down to survive.

I still needed cash for my trip, but I couldn't go to any of the places that used to carry Michael Vickers originals because Ancestor Lu's henchmen might be waiting for me there. There was no way the snooty galleries around Union Square were going to buy Dad's pictures of birds or diner scenes from the 1930s, so I drifted steadily toward a less expensive part of San Fran, passing the famous City Lights bookshop where the Beat Poets used to hang out, and rolling through the strange no man's land between Chinatown and Little Italy, where you can buy gelato in flavors like Green Tea, Lychee, and Quince.

I pulled into a random parking spot, locked the car and started pacing around the block, trying to collect myself. No easy matter: thoughts were bouncing around my brain as if my skull were a microwave and someone had left a pack of popcorn inside.

A yellow-rumped warbler came careening down the street and smacked squarely into the storefront window next to me. He dropped to the sidewalk in a heap. *Buddy*, I thought, darting over to see if he was okay, *I know just how you feel.* I could have sworn the warbler was a real bird with feathers and feet, sworn I heard the *tick*-SMACK of its beak meeting glass. But when

what kind of job could I possibly get in Texas?

Would it be good to have a Cunning Disguise™. Could I dye my hair? What color would be cute?

Who stopped the LJC guys under my window?

I hunched over the crumpled thing lying on the sidewalk, I found it was only origami, cunningly folded into taloned feet and twisted paper wings.

My eyes narrowed and I swung around, scanning the street for signs of a round-bellied, white-bearded, sly-eyed, smirk-mouthed, old Chinese guy with a fold-up donkey's head dangling out of his back pocket.

No sign.

If Paper Folding Man, that most eccentric of the Eight Chinese immortals, was around, he didn't want me to see him. Unless he was inside the building? I grabbed the paper bird and stashed it in my purse. Standing up, I took a look at the storefront the warbler had smacked into. The sign over the door said . . .

Lucky Larry's Used Waffle Irons—AND MORE!

The sign was painted in garish, carnival colors and framed by a pair of deeply disturbing clown heads. Looking through the dusty shop window I realized that Lucky Larry's was a sort of pawnshop with delusions of grandeur, and Larry himself was a collector with a peculiar taste for having things in sets. For instance, all the furniture had feet. No plain legs, no casters, no rollers. Feet. There was a bathtub with cast iron crocodile legs, a hat-rack with the carved wooden toes of an ostrich, a fat little ottoman with a dangling silk tail and the most unnervingly lifelike paws, so it looked as if someone had made it by stuffing a cocker spaniel. Similarly, the clocks all had *faces* for their faces, if you know what I mean: laughing babies, smiling sunflowers, mysterious Men in the Moon, pin-up girls from the 1950s, pious saints (lots of these), and sinister clowns (even more of them).

There were also paintings. Lots of them. Bad watercolor still-lifes of grapes and pears, blurry Impressionist café scenes of Parisians drinking coffee and eating croissant, a series of Expressionist things showing maggots crawling out of slabs of rotting meat, and an ancient oil painting of death's head and a bowl of fruit that looked so exactly like the Willem Claesz Vanitas that Lucky Larry had either commissioned a first-rate forgery, or stolen the original after bludgeoning its owner into unconsciousness with a vintage waffle iron. Personally, I was leaning to theory number two.

Looking at the paintings, I felt myself starting to smile for the first time all day. "Thank you, Paper Folding Man," I murmured, and I trotted back to the car for my dad's pictures.

Two minutes later I lugged my canvases into the shop. A bronze gong was mounted over the door; it ((((*bonged*)))) as I came inside, sending ripples of sound to seep into the dim interior like something spilled onto the many-footed furniture and disappearing into the upholstery, leaving behind only the insect sound of the clocks: the tick of pendulums, hands creaking as they crept around, and the tiny whirr and skitter of the gearworks forever scuttling out of sight. The place smelled of old books, varnish, leather, and dust. "Hello?" I called. "Anybody home?"

A portly man in his early 60s padded out from behind a Japanese screen whose feet were carved into turtles. He was wearing sandals, so I could see his toes were ornamented by long wiry loops of white hair that matched his shaggy white eyebrows and the white tufts that stuck out from his large ears. His blue jeans were hoisted up around his substantial belly by a pair of bright red suspenders, and he was wearing what looked like a Hawaiian shirt, except instead of brightly colored flowers, the print was a jumble of alarming clown-heads like the ones around the sign outside.

"Lucky Larry?" I guessed. I'm perceptive that way. "I was in the market for a used waffle iron."

"Really?" Larry hooked a pair of skeptical thumbs in his suspenders. "I would have guessed you wanted to sell me those paintings I see under your arm."

"I especially like my waffles with strawberries on them. Are there special waffle irons for that?"

"Because the whole idea of the shop is that customers give money to me," Larry explained. "Not the other way around."

We looked at one another. "So here's the thing," I said. "I need some cash." Lucky Larry sighed. "They're awfully good paintings." I pulled out the snowy egret. "Who wouldn't want that over their couch?" Larry shook his head. "Painting like this, an original Vickers oil painting, that's six, seven hundred bucks you can sell it for, easy!"

"Can't do it."

"You haven't even heard my price!"

Lucky Larry stuck a finger into one of his ears and wiggled it around, making the white hair rustle like jungle grass around an elephant's legs. "I only buy paintings of food."

I looked around the shop at the Expressionist pieces, maggots crawling out of steak. "Rotting meat counts?" He shrugged. "And what about that?" I asked, looking at the forged Claesz. "That's a skull, for crying out loud!"

"It's a bowl of fruit," Larry said, shaking his finger at me. "It just happens to be sitting *next* to a skull."

We locked eyes again.

"You could eat this," I said, waving at the snowy egret. "Look at the thighs on that thing. Yum!"

"Who eats cranes?"

"Snowy egret," I said automatically. "Is it edible? Heck, yeah! Slam it in the oven at 350, throw a little sherry on top . . . ." Larry looked dubious. "Or skewers," I said. "Egret Kabobs. It's the next big thing."

"I don't think—"

"Fondue!" I said desperately, as he started to shake his head again. "Who knows what kind of meat you're getting at those places? Cover it with Swiss cheese, nobody would know the difference."

"Listen, kid, I'd love to help," he said, sounding like he wasn't even a little bit interested in helping, "but I have a retail strategy here—"

"Furniture with hooves? That's a strategy?"

"—and I really have to stick with—"

"Owls," I said, going to the next painting.

"People eat owls?"

"All the time," I said. "The surgeon general says the American public needs at least two helpings of owl a week to . . . to . . . to encourage neck flexibility."

"Are a lot of American heads snapping off these days?"

"It's pretty alarming," I said.

Larry sidled behind the shop counter and turned to fuss with the hands on a clock with a hideous laughing clown on the face. "Thanks, but no thanks. Take a look around. I have a great little pig-themed dinette set— check out those hocks! They don't even make chairs like that anymore."

"They sure don't." I stalked over to the counter and leaning across it, willing the old man to turn around. "Listen—" I stopped in mid-rant as my eye fell on another painting stashed behind the counter. Blues and greys, tombstones, Hebrew letters carved into a stone pillar. *The Cemetery Gates*, by Marc Chagall.

"Anything in the store, I'll give you four percent off, just because I like you." Glancing over his shoulder, Larry saw my narrowed eyes and shuffled sideways to block my view of the painting.

"How much do you want for that?" I said, pointing at the Chagall.

"This? You don't want this," Larry said. "It's just a cheap reproduction. More like a poster, really."

"I'll give you a hundred bucks," I said. Mortally certain he was standing in front of the original Chagall—the painting Victor had bought half a year ago for six hundred thousand dollars, just because I mentioned it. "A

43.

hundred bucks, that's a great price for a cheap reproduction."

"Too much. I couldn't accept that, it would be wrong," Larry said. "Can I interest you in these lovely brass candlesticks in the shape of cows?" he said, putting a pair on the counter in front of me.

"Okay, then, I'll give you fifty bucks."

"To tell you the truth, I don't really want to sell this old thing," Larry said. "I've had it for ages—sentimental value—Aunt Ida—tragic spleen incident—unfortunate nursing home fire—I'm sure you understand."

"Oh, I understand." Because after all, Victor had woken up to find himself broke, right? And you can't sell a genuine Chagall to a reputable dealer for cash on the spot. You've got to have authentication and experts and insurance, and all those things take time. But if you needed a quick and dirty deal, cash on the barrelhead, Lucky Larry might be just the place to go. The shopkeeper and I locked eyes. "Name. Your. Price," I grated.

"Erm, well, I don't know . . ." He stared down at his hairy toes, then shrugged and looked back up. "Half a million?"

"I don't think I have that much on me."

"There's a surprise," Larry said dryly. "Listen, if the low-lifes around here had any idea how much the Chagall was worth . . . Let's just say I'd appreciate it if you didn't mention it to anyone, at least until I have time to buy a . . ."

"Safe?"

"Machine gun, I was thinking, but a safe would work, too." He frowned. "Do they make safes with feet?"

"*The Cemetery Gates* doesn't have any food in it."

Larry shrugged. "I made an exception."

I fingered the cow-shaped candlestick in front of me, trying to figure out how I could convince Larry to buy some of my dad's paintings. I picked up the candlestick. Hefted it. Violence, they say, is the last refuge of the incompetent.

Count me in.

"Larry," I said, getting a good grip on about four pounds of cow-shaped brass, "I bet you haven't had time to insure that painting."

He blanched and shuffled protectively in front of the Chagall. "You wouldn't."

I smiled whitely. "Try me." My fingers tightened around the candlestick, locking comfortably between its head and udders. Larry's whole torso began to shake and jiggle beneath his suspenders. "Or, maybe you'd like to reconsider buying a couple of my paintings?"

"Excellent idea!" he gasped. "So, I hear people are eating more owls these days."

"At all the best restaurants," I said.

Growing Up (Hour of Leaving Home)

I went home with one hundred and sixty dollars in my pocket. Enough to chip in some gas money for the trip, anyway, and buy Denny a bag of corn chips. Just before five o'clock Mom woke up while I was cooking (breakfast for her, dinner for me). She headed out to the hospital, and I washed dishes. My phone rang three times, Victor once and Emma twice, according to Caller ID. I didn't answer.

I was hoping that last night's massacre would discourage the Lucky Joy folks from coming back, but just in case I got the big knife from the kitchen, the one we used to carve roast (back when we could afford to buy roast). I was going to put it under my pillow, but the later it got the more obvious it was that I wouldn't be going to bed, so I just kept it on the desk next to my computer while I tried to write a note for my mom. Every half hour or so I would finish another version, stare at it, and then hit delete. There was nothing I could tell her, really. Nothing that wouldn't make her even more scared for me, even more convinced that I was on drugs or crazy or both.

I took out the letter Victor wrote to Tsao about me and read it over. I had treasured it for months, but this time I noticed all the spellings were British, and I realized it had been a fake from the start, something Tsao was using to get close to me.

Start dealing with immortals, you find a lot of fake things. A lot of lies.

http://www.doubletalkwireless.com/emmaslearningcurve/tsao.html

Victor Chan

I went to the closet and found the dress I had worn for our first real date, the time I dumped a crème brûlèe on Victor's head. I flipped through my sketchbook, looking at old pictures I had done of him, and Emma, and my mom. They were better than I remembered; not as good as I wanted them to be. Par for the course.

I found my eighth grade yearbook and flipped through to find Mrs. Saworski's class. **EMMA & CATHY, FRIENDS 4EVER** written in pink glitter pen by our pictures.

When dawn came I went outside. There were footprints in the grass, crossing the yard and circling the house like a sentry on patrol. Small feet.

Mom came home at 7:30 A.M. I made her breakfast. She was too tired to be suspicious. She staggered into the shower and then collapsed in bed, out like a light by 8:15.

Denny's car rolled up to the curb outside our house just before nine. I went into my room and grabbed the backpack with my laptop, sketchbook, and purse inside. I stopped in the bathroom to brush my hair because an artist never stops thinking about how she looks, and then I opened the front door and left the house I had grown up in, which I was never going to see again.

Denny's left arm was in a cast and a sling, tight against his chest. He reached awkwardly across his body and rolled down the driver side window. "Hey."

"Hey. Listen, why don't you let me drive?" I expected him to be macho and refuse, but his arm must have been hurting him pretty badly because he just nodded and fumbled awkwardly for the seat belt, trying to get it off with one hand. I leaned over and helped him with it. I could feel his breath, a little warm puff on the back of my neck as I reached across his chest.

He slid over to the passenger side. I dumped my stuff in the back seat, then got behind the wheel and turned the key. Rush hour was over and it was easy to get to the freeway. The cell phone in my pocket shuddered and rang, shuddered and rang. "You gonna get that?" Denny said.

I took the freeway entrance ramp and hit the gas, gaining speed.

"Nope."

I should have left a note.

Twins

"Why didn't you answer your phone?" Denny asked.

I shrugged. "I figure we stay on 101 for a sec, then take 92 over to 580 and go east until we can pick up I-5."

"Okay," Denny said. "Was it my sister calling?"

"Jewel? No. I mean, I didn't look." I glanced in the rearview mirror. No sinister panel vans with the Lucky Joy Cleaners logo on the side were following me. No cops. No sign of Mom, either, tailing me in our old Mercury Marquis. "We can take I-5 south as far as Bakersfield, maybe, and then cut west."

"Okay. Listen," Denny said.

"Then maybe catch 58 over by Tehachapi."

"Okay," Denny said. "There's a prison at Tehachapi," he added.

I glanced at the gas gauge. It was three quarters empty. "How many miles do you get to a gallon in this thing?"

"Sooner or later, she's going to call you back."

"Jewel?"

"When she does, I need you to get her number, okay? I need to talk to her."

"Did I tell you she took my driver's license?"

"She probably figured she—wait a sec. You're driving my car without a license?" Denny looked at the speedometer. "Slow down a little."

"I'm driving freeway speed!"

"Without a license," he said. "Slow down."

I got out of the fast lane and slowed down. "Why do you need me to get her number? Won't she call you herself? You guys seem pretty close." *In a weird, dysfunctional way.*

"She hates looking like a loser. We talk all the time when she thinks she's sitting in the catbird seat. It's when she gets quiet I know something's wrong. Then I have to figure out what's up right quick and bail her out. Which she hates," he added.

Talk about thankless jobs. Looking after an ungrateful Jewel had to rank somewhere between Itching Powder Tester and the guy who sweeps up after the circus elephants. "Are you the older one?"

"We're twins, but she actually beat me by two minutes. She always did want to see the world."

"I'm an only child."

"I could tell."

I looked over. "What does *that* mean?"

He was grinning. "Keep your eyes on the road, lady."

I found myself grinning, too. "Jerk."

With his good hand, Denny scratched absently around the top of the cast on his left arm, as if wishing he could scratch beneath the plaster. "My mom, she had this boyfriend when we were, like, seven. Lord, he was a hustler. He was gonna be somebody. So there was always this constant stream of buyers coming through the apartment, you know, coming to pick up their dope."

Ick. "Sounds like Jewel's awful taste in men runs in the family."

Denny shrugged. "He wasn't so bad. At least he was ambitious. Most of my Mom's boyfriends were just losers. He used to rent cool movies for us to watch, so we'd be quiet while he was dealing, you know? Stuff other kids didn't get to see."

"I'm afraid to ask."

"Oh, nothing with sex in it, he wasn't a pervert. *Nightmare on Elm Street,* stuff like that." I felt this stupid middle-class horror rising in my throat at the image of two little kids watching slasher flicks in the living room while the drug dealer boyfriend did his business at the kitchen table. And that was one of the *good* "fathers" in Denny's life.

Denny's face darkened. "There was this other guy, when Jewel was fourteen . . ." He looked down at his thick hand, scarred and stained with

48.

motor oil, knuckles a little swollen where they'd been broken, probably more than once. "I ran him off."

I drove the car.

"There's a lot of things you can see, even stuff you can do and still be a good person," Denny said. "As long as there is one other person in the world who knows you can be good." He turned away from me, looking out through the passenger side window as the highway slid into the past behind us. "Sometimes it feels like she's trying to get away from everyone who knows she can be good. Like, if she can get away from me, she can finally relax and just . . . be what everyone else thinks she is."

"But you're not going to let her go."

"No, ma'am," Denny said. "I surely don't mean to."

Windshield Buffet (Hour of the Movable Feast)

My phone rang. At first I was going to leave it in my pocket, but then I saw Denny looking at me so I dug the phone out and checked the caller ID. "Just Emma," I said, sticking it back in my pocket. "I wish she'd stop calling me."

"Should you maybe tell her where we're headed?" Denny said uncomfortably. "I mean, won't she be worried?"

"Thanks to me, Emma's dream company is down the toilet and hired killers are nosing around her apartment," I said grimly. "The last thing that girl needs is more Cathy in her life."

I caught Denny giving me a funny look. "Boy," he said brightly, "I sure am hungry."

"I've got about a hundred sixty bucks. With the price of gas the way it is, eating whatever hits the windshield might be about all we can afford."

Denny made a face. "Thanks for that image. Seriously, after two days of hospital food, I could go for a stack of flapjacks."

"You should have had a bigger breakfast." Of course, I hadn't managed to force down any food, either, and my stomach was starting to snarl. "We can stop at eleven and split a pack of peanuts or something, okay?"

50.

"You know, I believe I passed a pancake joint on my way into town. It ain't but a couple of miles down the road, here."

"Denny! We've been driving like eight minutes!" My traitorous stomach made a grinding noise like someone racing the engine on a cement mixer, only louder. "Now stop talking about food. It's just going to make us hungrier."

"Okay." He opened the glove compartment and flipped it closed, popped it open and flipped it closed. Like a mouth, a car mouth chewing on a big fat breakfast of instruction manuals. Open-close, open-close, yum yum yum yum. "Cathy," Denny said, "Don't you reckon a nice plate of flapjacks would—"

"What is with you and these pancakes, anyway?"

Denny's chunky face began to turn red. "I know you're going to be mad," he started.

"Oh my God, you need to pee. Right?"

"Um—"

"What are you, eight years old?" I snarled. "Fine! Just say so next time."

"Take this exit," he said gratefully.

"Men," I sighed.

Conquistador

Ring.

I glanced at Caller ID. At least it wasn't Emma this time; it was some guy named Miguel Allende. I frowned. There was something familiar about that name . . .

Ring.

Something shot up inside me up like a firework on the Fourth of July—a long hissing streak of breath followed by an explosion of memory. Miguel Allende was a conquistador, the guide on Ponce de Leon's doomed expedition to find the Fountain of Youth. Miguel Allende had drawn paintings of the New World, pictures of storks and mangroves and alligators. Pictures of a daughter left behind in Spain, because Miguel Allende was an immortal and when you're an immortal, a daughter is the kind of thing that gets left behind.

Ring.

"Cathy?" Denny said from over in the passenger seat. "Is that Jewel calling?"

"No," I said. "It's my dad."   I flipped the phone open. "Go to hell."

"I saw you leave this morning," my father said. "Who is that boy?"

"You've been watching the house? How very stalker of you."

"Cathy, don't be like this."

"He's human," I said, glancing at Denny. His blunt, half-ugly face was puzzled and concerned. "He's a nice, human boy and I'm running away with him. That's what you wanted, right?" My dad had made it very clear that he considered me and Victor a recipe for disaster. "Well, good news, I took your advice. Maybe in nine months or so I can be a one hundred percent-natural-human, unwed, teen mother. Aren't you thrilled, Dad?"

California girls spend so much time on our cell phones that we have evolved into basically a whole new race with special lobes of our brain entirely given over to distinguishing the kinds of silence people broadcast over their mobile devices. This was Type 113, "Weary, hurt, frustrated-but-long-suffering silence, with a secondary chord of guilt and lines of anguish in the upper frequencies." You get that one from parents a lot.

"Babies?" Denny blinked, still a couple of steps back. "Uh, I'm not sure I signed up for—"

"You stay out of this," I snarled. I took the freeway exit ramp and came to an intersection. "Which way do I turn to find your stupid pancake place?"

Rather than risk speaking, he just pointed.

My father said, "I heard about Ancestor Lu's men coming to the house."

"Wow, aren't you the concerned parent. So were you the one who left that trash under my window?" *Trash* here being a word meaning *corpses*.

"No, that wasn't me."

And stupidly, I was disappointed. *Sick, sick, sick Cathy.* It wasn't that I wanted my father to be a murderer. But it would have been bloody proof that he still cared and wanted to take care of us. "Well, at least you aren't a psychokiller, anyway."

"I've killed my share of people. And I would have killed these guys," my father said grimly. "In a heartbeat, if I had known they were trying to hurt you. But . . . I wasn't there."

"No. You sure weren't."

Silence #158. One of those parental silences whose ingredients I probably won't be able to name until I have children of my own, if I ever do. My father sighed. "Does your mother know about the bodies?"

"I don't think so."

"Good." He said, "Cathy, did you tell her you were leaving?"

"None of your business."

"You didn't even leave a note?"

I have no idea how he knew this. I said before I was a pretty good liar, but I could never fool Dad. I used to think it was because he knew me so well, but maybe it was just that he was such a practiced liar himself.

The car came up to an intersection and Denny pointed to the left. "Take this turn." He leaned over and stuck his stubbly face next to my phone. *"Mr. Vickers, just so you know, there's been no talk of babies, sir. Cathy just made that up."*

"Now, honey, don't be bashful. It's twins," I said loudly. "We're calling them Jeb and Bobby Sue."

"Cathy!" Denny and my father said at the same time.

"Your mother is going to be worried sick," Dad said.

"You know what? I'm making that your problem," I said. "You go over there and explain the whole situation to her, why don't you?"

"Cathy, this is stupid—"

"Actually, I think it's pure genius," I said. "Talk about killing two birds with one stone! She's going to be so mad at you, I'll just be an afterthought."

"Cathy!"

"Well, it's been great to catch up," I said brightly, easing the car into the parking lot of Helga's Pancake Hut. "Bye-bye now!"

bzzg buzz buzz bzzg
zzzzg

A Conspiracy Unmasked

I parked and we got out of the car. The day hadn't turned hot yet, but the taste of smoke seemed stronger, and the bright air was hazed with it, giving everything this bright Impressionist blur, as if someone had hired Monet to paint Helga's Pancake Hut right after he finished the Rouen Cathedral series.

"What you have to understand," Denny said nervously, "is that sometimes when people do things that make us angry, they were doing them for a really good reason."

"What are you babbling about?" I stalked across the parking lot to the restaurant door. The conversation with my father had left me fighting mad, but also feeling even more bitterly alone. I could add "Miguel Allende" to the list of Caller IDs I wouldn't pick up for, along with Emma, Pete, Victor, Mom, and everyone else I cared about. I'd take a call from Denny, maybe, for a few more days until I ditched him, too. And after that, who was left? Nice ladies from the phone company trying to sell me extra calling packages because they didn't know I couldn't talk to anyone anymore. Political candidates, wrong numbers, and . . . Jewel. And wasn't that worth a cold little smile; to think my life had come to a place where Jewel was the only call I would take.

Time to get rid of my phone, really. As Emma had proved so memorably six months ago, it was just a homing beacon the cops could use to find me. The cops . . . or Ancestor Lu's bounty hunters.

There was a trash can by the newspaper boxes outside the front door of the Pancake Hut. I stopped by it and took out my phone. It was another Emma special, a sweet little flip phone, Bluetooth-enabled and with a video camera capability I didn't know how to operate. I was pretty sure that Emma would have been able to use it to take battlefield MRI's, listen in on police radio, and fire tiny explosive crossbow quarrels, but in my hands it was just a phone and there was nobody I could talk to anymore. I dropped it in the trash, down into the barrel of half empty pop bottles, buzzing flies, old paper coffee cups, bits of newspaper, and leftover French fries. And smell, of course: the can was also brimming with the distinctive stench of stewing garbage.

Beep Beep Bzzz Bzz

Bzzz Beep Beep bring bring

"Hey," Denny said. "We could have sold that phone."

"Oh crap." I closed my eyes. After years of knowing Emma, I think of phones as something that just floats into your life for free, like smog. But of course even if I did want to get rid of the phone, it would be worth a little cash, and a little cash was a thing we really needed. Wrinkling my nose I peered back into the trash barrel with dismay.

"I think it slid under that dirty diaper," Denny said.

"Oh. Crap," I said again. I sighed and rolled up my sleeve.

"Wait! Hang on," Denny said, grabbing my arm with his one good hand. "Just—we'll take care of that in a second. Let's get inside. There's something I think you should see."

"A really long pair of tweezers?" I said morosely. "'Cuz that's about all I'm interested in."

He held the door to Helga's open for me with his one good arm. Say what you will about Texans, they do have nice manners. "What you have to understand is that after a life of bailing Jewel's ass out of trouble," Denny said, "sometimes I don't do exactly like I'm told."

A thick, terrible pressure started to clot in my throat as I walked into the Pancake Hut's dim, air-conditioned foyer. "Denny, what are you trying to tell me?"

The hand sticking out of his sling fluttered weakly, like a baby bird, but no actual words came out of his mouth. He looked into the restaurant and nodded at a round booth in the corner. The table was set for five but there were only three people there.

Emma was judiciously jiggling a teabag in a diner-issue, stainless steel teapot. She was wearing a standard Emma "business casual" outfit: blue jeans and a designer jacket over a Hello Kitty T-shirt. Next to her, Pete was scowling with concentration, adding one more level to the monstrous pyramid of creamers he had built to rise precariously on top of the napkin dispenser. Victor had his silver pocket watch in the palm of his hand. He glanced from its face up to mine with a faint smile playing over his mouth, as if he had timed my arrival to the second.

55

At that instant the knot in my throat got big as a fist, so I could hardly breathe. I know this feeling, I thought. This is trying not to cry.

"So, I didn't exactly keep your secret," Denny said. His bruised face was braced for impact, and I waited to see if I would slap him. I hoped I would. I hoped I was going to yell at him and turn on my heel and march out of there and stick to my plan, my perfectly logical plan to disappear. But the truth was, leaving my friends once had nearly killed me, and I knew in a heartbeat that I would never have the strength to walk out a second time.

Relief flooded into me. Relief and tearful gratitude and dizzy, knee-buckling joy. My body started to shake and I was crying after all, crying without tears, and for the first time in what felt like forever the crushing cloud of loneliness thinned a little and a ray of sunshine came in. Maybe my life wouldn't be a short, lonely, desperate chase with a brutal end after all.

Maybe everything would be all right.

"Denny?" I said, when I caught my breath, "I hate you."

His battered, lumpy face broke into a grin. "I know."

Emma

Emma was still fussing over her pot of tea as I walked up to the table. She loathed coffee and had absolutely no use for the kind of hot tea served in the average American restaurant; I knew from experience that she would have ordered a little stainless steel pot of boiling water, into which she would be dipping her own designer tea bag of some esoteric brew like "Flowers from the Jade Garden Jasmine Green" or "Imperial Phoenix Claw Oolong with Unicorn Shavings." She jiggled the teabag up and down, waiting until the water was the precise Seething Amber™ that signified Emma Tea Nirvana. She frowned at me over the tops of her little round glasses. "You're late," she said. Meaning:

- "The French toast I ordered for you is getting cold," and
- "Why the hell didn't you call me when you realized your life was on the line?" and

- "When are you ever going to understand that we are true friends, and as long as you have one true friend in the world you can never be really alone, even if every demon in the black legions of hell stands between us?"

"I'm sorry," I said, and "Thank you."
Meaning exactly that.

Victor

Victor stood up and grabbed me and gave me a hug. I could feel his relief in his hands, but I could feel how angry he was, too. How scared he had been. *I hurt him,* I thought wonderingly. Just by walking out my door I had managed to drive something through his heart that did more damage than bullets.

Time opened up, like it did when he touched me sometimes, and my heart stopped, and the wink and glint of silverware in the restaurant was like the play of light on water, and I could feel the muscles in his back and the warmth of his skin through the T-shirt he was wearing, and the smell of food crept right into my blood and I realized I hadn't been hungry for days but I was hungry now and the hunger was good because it meant I was alive.

Pete

Then time resumed and Pete looked speculatively at the bowl of creamers in front of my coffee cup. "Do you need those?"

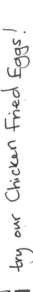

"The Cardiologist"
— Chocolate pancakes with Bacon Flavored Syrup!

Plan B

Five minutes later I was sitting with the people I loved best in the world and wolfing down slabs of diner French toast. "I am never trusting you again," I told Denny, spraying him with accusatory crumbs. "You promised you wouldn't tell."

"Don't blame Denny," Emma said briskly. "I dropped by the hospital yesterday afternoon and wormed it out of him."

"I've been wormed by Emma," Pete said, adding another creamer to his pyramid. "—Nasty."

"When I dropped by last night I didn't have to do any worming at all," Victor said. "He just upped and told me you were going to make a break for it."

"I read about it on the Internet," Pete added.

"Ha, ha." Denny said. "Thanks, guys. You're really helping me out, here." He was sheepish enough to avoid my eyes, keeping his attention strictly fixed on his enormous breakfast. Victor had said he was paying, and Denny had ordered like a man who might never get another meal, some 9000-calorie monstrosity off a page of the menu obviously designed for sumo wrestlers, pythons, or hibernating bears.

Victor shook his head at the vast mound of food steadily disappearing down Denny's throat, then grinned at me. "See? Now Denny likes me better than you."

"You do have better legs," I admitted.

"You know what they say about the quickest way to a man's heart," Pete said.

Emma looked up quizzically. "Through his chest?"

Pete looked nonplussed. "Were you raised by werewolves or something?" Emma bared her small white teeth and snarled prettily at him.

God, they were cute. *Were — Emma!*

I emptied little plastic cuplets of half-and-half into my cup of diner coffee: one, two, three of my own and a fourth one filched heartlessly from the top of Pete's pyramid. "Guys, Ancestor Lu is going to keep coming for me until he sees me lying face down in his freezer with a tag around my toe. The only way you can ever be safe is if I disappear."

try our Chicken Fried Eggs!

57.

everybody loves Candied Strawberries in beef gravy!

58.

"You'll never disappear enough," Victor said. "Sooner or later he's going to find you."

Emma was using her knife and fork to cut her bacon into small squares. "Nothing you can do can keep us safe."

"Thanks for that, Little Miss Sunshine. Look, what if I change my name to Mary Jo?" I said. "Be a waitress at a donut shop. Take up bowling and collect country & western music."

Pete had paused long enough in his pyramid construction to be attacking his breakfast, a big bowl of granola. I didn't know they even served granola in diners. He shook his head, munching wetly on Nature's Bounty Steel Cut Oat Flakes with Coconut-Almond Clusterettes. "It's not like the old days," Pete said between mouthfuls. "It's hard to disappear now. Even I could track you, if I was willing to break the law. I know your credit card info. I could follow the gas station receipts, figure out where you are. Wait until the purchases settle down in one city."

"I don't have to use a credit card," I said uncomfortably, thinking of the one hundred and sixty dollars in my back pocket. That wasn't going to last very long.

"When you apply for that job in the donut shop, you'll have to provide a social security number."

"I could work just for cash—trade my paycheck for someone else's tips."

Pete shrugged. "If you want to open a bank account, or get the gas turned on in your apartment, you have to show legal ID."

"You can't convince me it's impossible. For God's sake, half the people in San Jose are illegal immigrants."

"Sure, but those people are living with family. If you have two real IDs, that's plenty enough to get gas and water and power and school records organized for ten others. Plus the feds aren't tracking down one particular chica: whereas Ancestor Lu wants you, personally, and he wants you bad." Pete spread out his hands. "I'm not saying it's impossible to drop off the data grid . . . but it's hard."

Emma looked at me over the edge of her tea cup. "The other problem with your plan," she pointed out "is that as a waitress, you suck."

"So what am I supposed to do?" I stared around the table. "If I can't disappear, and I can't stop the bad guys from killing me, am I just supposed to throw myself off the Golden Gate Bridge and save them the cost of the bullet? Honestly, Em, I hope you've got a Plan B for dealing with Ancestor Lu."

Emma looked at me in surprise. "Isn't it obvious? We have to kill him."

Death and Weddings

"Kill him!" I said loudly.

A plump woman in the next booth turned around and stared at me in surprise. I was in no mood to be chastised by anyone in a strawberry-colored pantsuit, so I glared at her, and she turned back to her table, her back radiating stiff disapproval. *"Kill him?"* I hissed.

"We've talked this through quite thoroughly," Emma said reassuringly.

"When?"

"Last night in Denny's hospital room."

Emma, Pete, Victor, and Denny all plotting and planning together? "Without me?"

"You rather uninvited yourself," Emma said dryly.

Either one of Denny's bruises had ruptured or he was actually starting to blush. "We figured if we said anything last night, you might just split before we had a chance to get organized. This way . . ."

"You could just pick me up like a package and deliver me. Fine! I give up!" I waved my fork around. "Don't say I didn't try to keep you out of this."

"We don't want out," Victor said. We're your friends, and we'll stick by you no matter what."

"Dummy," Emma added.

Victor spread out his hands. "As for Ancestor Lu, we have to neutralize him. If there's a way to do it without killing him, I'm all for it, but it's bad tactics to sit around waiting for him to make the next move."

Pete had finished his granola and was making a little catapult with his

59.

spoon, putting a sugar packet on the handle and then whacking the bowl so the sugar went flying over his pyramid of creamers. "Could we persuade him to just go back to China?"

"I still like the killing option," Emma said, "but that's just me."

"Whoa. Since when did you go all Slayer on me, Buffy?"

"Since you found dead hit-men up under your window and I saw live ones circling around my apartment."

I gulped. Pete nodded. "I rigged a camera. There's no doubt about it. They were staking out her place."

"Waiting for you," Victor said.

"The first thing we need to do is make a list of our assets." Emma pulled a typical piece of twenty-third-century Emmaware out of her purse, some kind of PDA/laptop hybrid that was probably worshipped as a god by certain microwave ovens and flat screen TVs. She flipped it open like a switchblade and summoned a file by making mystical passes over the high-res screen and chanting something in what might have been ecclesiastical Latin. "I've started a spreadsheet of our current resources, broken down by category. Anything tangible is dark, intangibles are light, social resources are blue, facilitative tech is brown, money and financial assets are green, obviously, and weapons, naturally, are red." She looked around the table to make sure we were all following. "So, for instance, under Paper Folding Man, I have his donkey listed in dark brown, as a tangible transportation asset, whereas his ambient goodwill is a social intangible, listed here in light blue." She tilted her head to one side and frowned. "Although, the goodwill of an immortal is probably worth more than the good will of a regular person, so I should probably darken that entry by twenty percent." She looked up. "Does that make sense?"

Pete was grinning. "Awesome."

"Maybe I just missed something while I was in hospital," Denny said, jabbing a forkful of his Hash-Browns-Ham-Scrambled Egg-Cheese-Butter-Bacon-Gravy-'N-Syrup Skillet, "but didn't you say this dude is immortal? How do you kill him? Drop him into a volcano?"

"It worked for Frodo," Pete pointed out.

"There's a serum that can make the immortals vulnerable," Victor said. "Ancestor Lu developed it from some research I was doing for him. That's how . . ." He trailed off.

"Right. That's what Jewel did to the dude that broke my arm," Denny said. "Before she shot him."

There was a sudden awkward silence. Did Denny even realize Tsao was Victor's father? Emma and Pete both looked sharply at Victor. I was ashamed to realize I hadn't even really thought about how Victor was dealing with Tsao's death. The two hadn't been close, obviously; Tsao had abandoned the family as the immortals always did. Victor had never known him as a boy; last winter they had met for the first time in a hundred and twenty years.

But as I had reason to know, having a father die does strange things to your heart.

My mom talked about it, just a little, when her mother passed away. "It's not just the person you've lost," she told me. "As long as your parents are alive, it's like living in a house. There's a wall between you and the outside. But when they die, a door opens, and there's nothing between you and death any more."

I looked at Victor. His face looked so young and his eyes looked so old. I wondered if Tsao's death had him thinking more about his other families, the women he had loved and the children he had fathered before he ever met me. After WWII he had lived for a time in French Indochina with a woman named Giselle. I wondered if he had loved her more than he loved me. I wondered how often he thought of her now.

How strange it must be, waiting at the altar on your wedding day, seeing your bride walk towards you on her father's arm, knowing that your marriage is really just a pause, a waiting period, until Death comes to walk her back down the aisle.

Much Ado about Cash (Hour of the Empty Pockets)

"What would it take for you to manufacture the serum?" Emma asked Victor.

"A lot," Victor said frankly. "I wasn't on the team that developed it. I have some pretty good guesses as to what they did, but Lu has all my notes. Plus it would take some pretty expensive equipment."

"How expensive?"

Victor started ticking things off on his fingers. "A thermal cycler to do the PCR, and that's fifteen grand right there. An ultracold freezer, tabletop centrifuge, small autoclave—that's another ten grand. Incubator, electrophoresis setup, reagents, pipettes, other glassware . . ." Victor shrugged. "Seventy-five thousand dollars, maybe? Sixty-five if you went to the Gene Therapy aisle at ShopMore."

Seventy-five thousand dollars. "Ouch," I said.

Emma looked unhappily at her spreadsheet. "I know how much money Pete and I have to put in the war chest. Victor?"

"About two thousand dollars."

"What?" I squawked. "Didn't you hock the Chagall?"

"How did you know that?"

"A little bird told me." Quite literally true in this case, if magic origami yellow rumped warblers count.

"I pawned it, I didn't actually sell it outright. And that's where a thousand bucks came from."

"The wine in your house alone must be worth—"

Victor shook his head. "Lu's people removed all the valuables while I was working in his bunker. Collateral against my good behavior, they said." He took out his skeleton watch and glanced at the hands. It was just past ten in the morning. Like a head with the skin taken off to show the skull, there was no face on Victor's watch, so beneath the hands the naked gears clicked and whirred, measuring out, second by second, the passing of a time that meant nothing to him—a tiny mechanical heartbeat that would wind down

a tiny scientific piano

for raising immortal chickens

cutting edge scientific instrument for hair removal.

62.

where his flesh and blood never would. Victor held up the watch. "This is the only thing I've got left to sell."

"So you have two thousand," Emma said, entering into her spreadsheet. "Let's leave the watch out of it for now. Denny?"

Denny reached into his pocket and counted out a crumpled heap of bills and change. "Two hundred seven dollars and fourteen cents."

Emma entered the numbers into her PDA and made a face. "What are we short?" I asked.

"About . . . sixty thousand dollars."

"Oh," I said. My one hundred and sixty dollars suddenly didn't seem worth mentioning.

"I could sell my boat," Pete suggested. "The *Moonshine* must be worth..."

"Twenty thousand?" Emma suggested. "Fifteen? I think we're still a little short."

"So our first priority is making money," Pete said, grinning at Emma. "How refreshing." Emma gave him a wry smile.

"Our first priority is finding a place to stay where Ancestor Lu can't track us down," Victor said. "Buying a few groceries wouldn't hurt, either."

"We can stay on the boat," Pete said. "If you guys don't mind sleeping three in the cabin, I can sleep on the deck . . ."

". . . and Victor can hang upside down from the mast like a vampire bat!" I said. "Or there's Option B, a cheap motel."

Emma sighed. "We're going to have to raise some venture capital. We need a business plan for some kind of biotech start-up. We might be able to fast track negotiations with a VC, give away most of our equity and get a half-million dollar seed round," she murmured. "Maybe there's something, a tissue sample from Victor or something that we could show to justify the rush. . ."

"How long would that take?" I asked.

"If everything breaks right . . . three months?" Emma said. "More likely six before the money hits the bank. But what other choices do we have?"

"White collar crime?" Pete suggested.

"No!" Emma threw a packet of sugar at him.

"Identity theft," he said cheerfully, undeterred. "Credit card fraud. The possibilities are endless."

"I don't wish to go to jail, thank you very much!"

"Jail sucks," Pete said mildly, "but it beats the morgue."

"There is another way," I said reluctantly.

Pot of Poison—Remix

Everybody turned to look at me. "I have some of the serum."

"What!"

"Why didn't you tell us?" Emma asked. Victor just looked at me.

I flushed and felt that numb, buzzing feeling you get in your body when someone catches you doing something shameful. I should have told them sooner. "The serum spray was in Jewel's perfume bottle. That's how she got the stuff on Tsao. Right after she shot him, she went to the bathroom to throw up, and I took it out of her purse."

Denny licked the gravy off a Chicken Fried Sausage Patty with renewed enthusiasm. "Rock on, Cathy."

"A free silver bullet," Pete said. "Or maybe wooden stake. Vial of holy water? Clove of garlic?"

"We got it," Emma said. She reformatted her spreadsheet, humming a happy spreadsheet song. "That certainly represents a considerable savings in time and money."

"Seems like a funny thing not to mention." Victor's voice was mild, but his eyes were sharp.

"It wasn't a big deal," I muttered, looking down at my plate. "It was crazy, everything was happening so fast."

"She never saw anybody get killed before," Denny said.

"And it wasn't exactly something I was proud of," I added. "Stealing something out of Jewel's purse."

"Yes, I know how you feel about stealing."

64.

The feeling of being caught in a lie intensified. I had broken into Victor's house, not once but two times, and taken things from it, as he knew perfectly well. I had broken into his lab back when he worked at Intrepid Biotech, for that matter. I stole stuff then, too.

"I think you just liked having this stuff," Victor said. "A magic bullet especially for immortals. A way to get even." His eyes wandered slowly over to Denny and then back. "Another way to get even."

"What the hell does *that* mean?" I said hotly. Grateful to be pissed off because it sure as hell beat feeling ashamed.

"You tell me." Victor's lithe body was tense, quick, sharp. I'd seen him this way before, spoiling for a fight. "You decide you're going to disappear, because after all you need to protect us," he drawled. "So you run away from your smart friend and your hacker friend and your boyfriend, the one who—supposedly—can't be killed. You leave all of us behind and instead. . ." He jerked his head over at Denny, sitting across the table in his cast and his clown's face of bruises. "Instead you sign up for a cozy little road trip with the one person who has *proved* he can't protect you from Ancestor Lu in any way at all."

"Shut up!" Denny said, lunging at him. "I'll kick your ass into the middle of next—"

Victor effortlessly caught Denny's clumsy off-balance punch and twisted his wrist over into a joint-lock. Denny's face slammed into the table, and he lay with his breath coming in little pained gasps. The pyramid of creamers on the napkin dispenser collapsed and little caplets of imitation half-and-half skittered across the table.

"Victor!" I glared at him. "Stop being a jerk!"

The plump blond lady turned around again to glare at us.

"Come on, Kung Fu," Denny said through gritted teeth. "Break my hand. That will totally impress Cathy. Chicks dig that stuff."

"Stop talking," Victor said.

"Seriously, dude. Does she even *like* you?" Denny's face paled as Victor tweaked his wrist. He grinned raggedly. "She likes me, I'll tell you that."

65.

"Shut up! Both of you!" I yelled.

Pete grabbed Victor by the shoulder. "Dude. Lay off." He jerked Victor's shoulder around, hard, until he got eye contact. "That's enough."

Victor closed his eyes, nodded, let go. "He swung at me first," he muttered.

"Take the testosterone somewhere else, both of you," Emma said sharply. Victor mastered himself. "You're right." He looked straight at Denny. "That was wrong of me. It was contemptible."

"What? Hitting the cripple?" Denny grabbed a napkin with his one good hand and wiped off his shirt where it had been pressed into his food. "Don't patronize me, Prince Charming."

"Don't you go dragging me into your peeing contest," I told Denny. "This isn't about me."

"Yes, actually, it is," Victor said tightly. "It's about you, and me, and your dad."

"This *really* isn't about my father—"

"*It's about nothing else*," Victor snapped. He forced himself to stillness. "Cathy, yes, I am immortal. But I am not the man who walked out on you."

"Yet," I said.

We glared at one another across the table, and then Victor's shoulders slumped. "What is it going to take, Cathy? What do I have to do to make you trust me? Drop dead?"

"Well, it would be a good start."

Victor looked away. He pulled out his pocket watch again and held it in his hand, watching the clockwork beat out its steady mechanical pulse. "Maybe I should do just that."

"Cathy?" Denny reached over and touched the back of my hand. "You okay?"

I jerked my hand away. My eyes felt hot and hard and my cheeks were burning. "I've got to go pull a phone out of the trash," I said, scooting out of the booth and leaving my purse behind. "I'll be right back."

Garbage Clean Up (Hour of the Plus Size Assassin)

I dug the phone out of the garbage in front of the Pancake Hut and then went into the bathroom, mostly to wash my hands but also because I wasn't ready to face the others yet. I had slept about four hours over the last two days, for one thing; pure fatigue was beginning to leave my stitching a little ragged along the emotional hems. And strangely enough, just seeing my friends made everything harder. I had screwed up my courage to get lost, and as glad as I was to be found instead—and I was deeply, tearfully grateful to see them all waiting in the Pancake Hut waiting for me—it was as if the moment I relaxed just a little, all that courage had sort of drained away , like syrup disappearing into my French toast.

I was splashing cold water on my face when I heard someone else come into the Ladies' Room. My face was dripping, which was good, as it hid the tears that had been playing hell with my mascara pretty much the whole time since I left Victor and the others at the table. I don't like it when people know I've been crying.

I snuck a look in the mirror to see who had come into the bathroom, fearing it was going to be Emma determined to Have a Talk, but it wasn't Emma. It was the disapproving woman from the next booth. *Of course*, I thought. A little MORE disapproval: just what I needed. I snuck another glance. She was a large woman wearing a strawberry-colored pant suit, with a plump face but a sharp nose that made me think irresistibly of a 200 lb version of the Little Red Hen. Big Honking Red Hen.

Big Honking Red Hen was rooting through her purse as if looking for a compact or a lipstick. I started to reach for a paper towel to dry my face. My eye skimmed across BHRH's reflection in the bathroom mirror and then stopped, quivering like a dart in a dartboard, at a tiny metallic gleam from deep inside the folds where her ketchup-colored shirt met her impressive bosom. She was wearing a silver chain around her neck, and peaking out of the top of her blouse I could just see the dull round edge of some kind of pendant. It was bronze-colored. About the size of a coin.

67.

68.

My heart stopped. I waited for it to start again but it seemed to be taking its sweet time, so I figured I might just have to work without it. *Act normal,* I told myself. *Don't do anything to draw attention.* Ignoring this excellent advice, instead I gave an involuntary squeak of fear and dove into the nearest bathroom stall, slamming the door shut behind me.

Whoops. So much for acting normal.

I heard a rattle as Big Crimson Chicken pulled something large out of her purse. Possibly a lipstick the size of a can of spray paint. More likely a gun. Hunched on top of the toilet seat, I ducked my head and peered at the sliver of floor visible under the stall door. A pair of low-heeled raspberry pumps appeared outside my cubicle. I thought about turning the lock but that seemed like it might take actual coordination, whereas the only thing I had going for me was a fire-hose-sized blast of adrenaline, so I kicked the stall door back open as hard as I could.

There was a satisfying metallic CRANG and an even more satisfying string of cuss words from Big Red. She went staggering back into the Formica countertop clutching her nose, which I very much hoped was broken. Her gun went clattering into the far sink, the one under the Coin-Operated Feminine Hygiene Product Dispenser.

I lunged for the bathroom door, but Kentucky Fried Woman wheeled into a karate kick that would have made Bruce Lee proud, driving her tacky red pump into my stomach. I folded like a cheap accordion, gasping for air. Big Red's follow-up was a roundhouse slap with her fat ring-encrusted hand. This I cleverly blocked with my ear before pinwheeling to the floor.

The tile was cool and hard against my face.

I rolled away from another kick and scrambled madly backwards until I hit my head, hard, on the aluminum garbage can where the used paper towels went to die. I sat there bleeding quietly inside my mouth while an interesting black fog gathered in front of my eyes and then slowly began to disperse. ChickenZilla crouched down in front of me in a creak of polyester. I figured out she had gotten her gun back when she shoved the barrel between my teeth. "Okay, sweetheart," she clucked, in the exact voice of my third grade teacher. "When I count to three, say 'cheese.' One . . ."

The gun was hard in my mouth, grinding against my teeth. It tasted like darkness. Then, as if in slow motion, the bathroom door swung open behind Big Red. At first I thought this was just a subjective experience, my life flashing before my eyes as I faced death, but time kept stretching out like cold syrup dangling from a bottle, slowing down in that familiar way that signaled an immortal arriving on the scene.

And then the gun was gone, and Henny Penny was flying backwards, fantastically hard, to smash into the bathroom mirror. Glass splintered, popped, and toppled off the wall, raining around her in slow motion, and Ancestor Lu's daughter, Jun, was standing in the Ladies' Room at Helga's Pancake Hut. She was dressed all in white, her thin elegant figure beautiful and deadly, her long black hair swinging like the tassel on the pommel of a sword.

Time started again.

I gaped. "What the hell are you doing here?"

The chubby would-be assassin was cringing in her pool of broken glass. Jun studied her the way you might look at a crippled wasp before stepping on it. Big Red's eyes widened as Jun slid a slim ivory-handled knife out of her sleeve. "She was at your house, watching you. I was watching her." Jun stepped lightly across the bathroom floor. Her feet, dainty in china flats, whispered among the splinters of broken glass. Holding the knife in her right hand she grabbed Red's hair in her left. "Lean forward," she said, and she jerked the woman's head forward so her throat was over one of the sinks.

"No!" I cried.

Big Red's eyes were wide with terror. A vein in her throat throbbed with her pulse, pushing against the razor-sharp knife Jun held lightly against her skin.

"No?" Jun said, puzzled. Her thin, perfect eyebrows rose. "Why not?"

I licked my lips. "I don't know. But don't. It's wrong."

Jun tilted her head, considering. "You would not let me kill Little Sister. That time, I think you were right." She glanced at the plump Lucky Joy operative cringing away from the knife at her throat. A piece of glass had cut Big Red under one eye and a trickle of blood was creeping down her cheek

like a red tear. "Little Sister did not deserve to die. This one does."

I pulled myself up, shaking my head. "God protect us all from getting what we deserve." I picked up Big Red's gun.

Her eyes widened. "Please. I got a family. It was nothing personal, swear to God."

My hands were shaking and the gun was pointing at her chest. "It was pretty damn personal to me." Big Red watched me, terrified, waiting to see if I would pull the trigger. I was kind of curious about that myself. I had never wanted to kill anyone before. But right now, with the massive dose of adrenaline screaming through my blood, I wanted to hurt her. I wanted to make her pay for making me so scared.

I took a deep breath and put the gun down beside her purse. "Here's what you are going to do, Little Red Hen. You are going to leave here today and never come back."

"But I got a condo in—"

Jun tapped Red's throat with the edge of the ivory-handled knife. The woman's mouth snapped shut. "You be quiet," I hissed, still shaking, "or I swear I will let this lady do exactly what she wants."

Red looked at Jun and read quick death in her eyes. She swallowed. Beads of sweat were springing up all over her round face. "I'll do anything you want," she whispered.

I started going quickly through Big Red's purse. "You're going to move to another part of the country," I said. "To a state that begins with the letter I."

"The letter I," she said dutifully.

I pulled out her wallet and rifled through it. Three different driver's licenses under three different names. A couple of credit cards, a grocery store Customer Rewards card, a Triple A card and something from the San Jose Public Library. "There you will change your name to Mary Jo—"

"Mary Jo. Got it."

"And get a job in a donut shop."

"Donut shop." Kentucky Fried Woman shook her head, confused. "Does it have to be a donut shop?" she asked timidly, "or would a bakery be okay?"

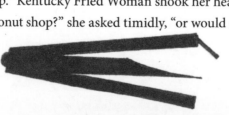

"Bakery is fine." I pulled the money out of her wallet. Eighty-four dollars and change. I took forty bucks and Big Red's real driver's license, the one that matched the library card, along with a credit card in the same name and her Social Security card. I left the rest of the stuff in her wallet. I shoved the wallet back in her purse and then leaned in, jabbing her in the collarbone with my finger. She cringed backwards, as if trying to scramble back through the wall. A few more pieces of broken glass fell clattering to the countertop. "Do you think the people who hired you are scary?" I asked. Wordlessly she nodded. "Then maybe you should ask yourself why they're so scared of me."

"I'm most scared of her," Red said apologetically, flicking a scared glance at Jun.

"I believe someone in the restaurant heard us. They're calling the police," Jun remarked casually, as if it wouldn't bother her in the least to lay waste to the entire San Jose Police Department should the occasion require it.

For their sake, I figured it was time to go.

Sticks & Stones (Hour of Cool's Death Rattle)

We cleared out of Helga's in a hurry. Victor and I still had unfinished business, obviously, but with broken glass and blood in the Ladies' Room behind us, and who knew how many more Lucky Joy agents lurking around, there was general agreement that we had better shelve our personal problems for a few hours and concentrate on staying alive. I grabbed my purse from the booth, checking to make sure the perfume bottle was still inside, and then hightailed it out to the parking lot, where we all agreed to follow Pete to a place he said would be perfect for holding a council of war.

Sticks & Stones

"Your Truck Stop on the Information Superhighway"

"Isn't this place great?" Pete enthused as we walked inside. He and Emma were in front; me next, with Denny shuffling behind, gazing around appalled at the yuppification of everything he held dear. The immortals brought up the rear: Jun like Death in china flats, Victor if anything more jittery than he had been before. His eyes darted around in the oddest way, like a man just waking up and finding the world is suddenly new and strange to him.

"It's the most technologically advanced pool hall in the world!" Pete enthused. "Check this out!" He pointed out the closed-circuit cameras hanging over every pool table, relaying footage to nearby flat-screen monitors that replayed each shot in super slo-mo. Sprinkled around the tables and in front of the bar were about a dozen guys, all wearing slacks or khaki shorts and sporting Regulation Software Engineer Short Sleeved Shirts. Most of them were drinking mineral water or diet soda, although a couple sported bottles of microbrewery beers with names like "Amorous Armadillo Lager." Hair ranged from messy to moussed, with a lot of male pattern baldness, and almost every dude was sporting some kind of beard, ranging from Terrorist Stubble to Late 1990s goatees, with a couple of unfortunate early Klingon beards and one full Mountain Man bush. Most of the guys seemed to have blue chalk stains on their shirts, and as far as I could tell none of them could play a lick.

"Jesus H. Christ," Denny whispered, looking around in shock. "They killed pool!"

72.

"These guys have *everything*," Pete continued happily, grabbing a table by the bar and plugging a power cord into a socket built into its base. "Power anywhere you sit, hot and cold running Wi-Fi, and every flavor of Mexican pop known to man—including lime, mango, watermelon, and tamarind."

"Tamarind?" Denny said faintly, still staring around and scrunching up his bruised face.

"It's a fruit. Or possibly a spice?" Emma said helpfully. "It's what makes Worcestershire sauce taste like Worcestershire sauce."

"Worcestershire-sauce flavored pop?" Denny closed his eyes. "The only flavors you should ever get in a pool hall are blood, tears, motor oil, and beer."

"Yeah, well, welcome to civilization," Pete said cheerfully. He plugged in his laptop and flipped it open. "We're just a couple of blocks from the big Adobe campus, and right down the street from CISCO systems. Muscle means something a little different here."

"Un-hunh," Denny said disbelievingly.

Pete grinned. "See that dude over there?"

"The fat guy in the Yoda T-shirt who just sank his cue ball?"

"When he was fifteen, he shut down the entire Department of Health and Human Services with a DNS attack after his mom's rent went up. He was too young to be tried as an adult, so the judge sent him to three months of juvie, and when he got out he dropped out of tenth grade because he got a job in counter-security with a starting salary of two hundred grand a year."

Denny blinked.

"You can buy a lot of Yoda action figures for two hundred thousand dollars," Emma said thoughtfully.

"So what does that make you, killer?" Victor said, grinning strangely. "Are you a hustler in this world, Pete? Are you a stone cold cyber-gangsta?"

"I have some game," Pete said absently, watching his machine boot up. "Cathy, give me the ID you took from the woman who jumped you."

I fished out Big Red's ID. "What are you going to do with it?"

Pete pointed his browser at www.luckyjoycleaners.com. "The first order password protection on this site is pretty weak. I'm betting a standard

73.

dictionary search and a little bit of patience will get me inside. But what I really want is to get server side on them, so I can start sniffing their internal communications." Pete's voice sank to a murmur as he squinted at his screen. "For that kind of hack, having some data on a registered user will save us some time."

Victor prowled around the table. "Is this going to take long?" Pete shrugged. "I'm going to go play pool, or—God, I'd love a beer! I haven't had beer in . . . ." He stopped, shook his head and smiled, like a man talking to himself. "In what feels like forever." Turning on his heel he marched over to the bar. Jun watched him go. I watched Jun.

"Let's play pool," Emma said, grabbing me by the wrist. "Pete's going to be a while."

"Shouldn't we stay and help him break the law or something?"

Emma gave me a look. "Cathy, you've had zero sleep in the last thirty hours and you still don't know how to program the speed dial on your phone." She pulled me to my feet. "I imagine Pete will scrape by without your technical assistance."

Perfume for Two (Hour of the Secret Stash)

Emma and I playing at one table, Victor and Jun at the next: Denny sitting on a stool between the two, his damaged arm in its sling cinched tight to his chest, his stubby hand gripping a bottle of regular beer like a shipwrecked man would hold on to a piece of wreckage to keep from drowning.

Emma was taking what seemed like a very long time to set up our balls. Finally she trotted back to the other end of the table and set up the cue ball. "Thank God," I murmured. But Emma paused, frowning back at the triangle of solids and strips. "Now what?"

"They're not quite centered," she said, heading back.

"Emma! Nobody cares if the triangle is perfectly equilateral!"

"Blasphemer."

I gritted my teeth.

A few feet away from me, at the next table over, Jun was preparing to break. She bent low over the ball, cold and beautiful as a knife blade, sighting along the line of her cue. She went completely still—her long hair glossy and black as if carved out of obsidian; her pale skin eternal as winter; her eyes as empty as stars. Slowly, slowly she drew her hand back, each millimeter slower as if she was pushing back gravity, or time, until finally the perfect stillness at the back of her stroke. And then time released, the hand loosed like an arrow, the white ball hitting the mass of stripes and solids like a grenade fired into a nest of marbles. Balls rocketed out from the impact, whining and smacking into one another, clattering all around the table, and then dropping into pockets, one, two, three of them, all solids.

"Nice *shot*." Denny contemplated a mouthful of beer. "Um, we haven't actually been introduced . . ."

Jun ignored him. "Sorry," I said. "This is Jun, Ancestor Lu's daughter."

"Daughter?" Denny studied her with renewed interest. "Hm."

"Four in the corner pocket," Jun said coolly. She bent to the table: time stopped. *Crack. Bam. Plop.*

Denny considered. "She's one of Them."

"Yep," I said loudly. "They make a lovely couple, don't they?"

*

Emma broke (sort of) but didn't sink anything, making it my turn. At the next table Jun was lining up her third shot, but Victor was ignoring her and ostentatiously watching mine. I tried hard to ignore him, but I could feel his eyes on me as if someone was pushing two hot marbles into my back. I bent over the cue ball and jabbed at it in a sudden, violent, and flustered fashion, like a woman poking a broom handle into a wasp's nest. The tip of my cue went low, ripping the felt and burrowing underneath it.

"Whoa. Trick shot!" Victor held his beer up in a mock salute to the flat-screen monitor overhead as it replayed the shot in exquisitely embarrassing slow motion. I felt my face begin to burn.

75

It was barely eleven o'clock in the morning, and it was already turning into a very long day.

Emma stood next to me, surveying the table. "So Jun must have been the one who left those bodies under your window," she murmured.

I watched Jun and Victor play, all speed and precision, circling the table in a kind of Pool Hall Tango, Victor with his silver watch chain swinging at his hip, Jun's long black hair rustling like silk with every move. "God I hate her hair," I muttered. "Who am I kidding? Look at them. They're perfect together."

"Oh, perfect." Emma cuffed me lightly in the head. "Except Victor loves you instead."

"Maybe. For now." I made one of my mom's noises, the little skeptical *Meh* she would make when promised that taxes would go down or my grades would go up. "In twenty-five years, I will look like my mother. In fifty years, I will look like *his* mother."

"Ew!"

"—and that lady died in about 1910, so she isn't the hottest thing in pantyhose anymore."

Emma made another hapless attempt to sink a striped ball. "Your turn." She snuck a peek over at the other table. "I don't think Jun's looks are anything so special," she added loyally.

"Are you kidding me? She was probably the cover of the *Sports Illustrated* swimsuit issue in 1628." I snuck another look at Jun as she bent over to line up a shot—the fall of her hair, the severe beauty of her eyes and mouth, the lean body that shifted beneath her clothes. "No, speaking purely as an artist, that is a beautiful woman." I took aim at the four ball and hit it really hard to nowhere in particular, figuring it was bound to fall into a pocket sooner or later if it just kept rolling long enough. This turned out not to be true.

"She isn't very *fun*," Emma said under her breath. "And I think calculus is amusing, so I am pretty easy to please."

"I'll give you that," I admitted. "Her mom didn't send her to school with a sense of humor in her lunch sack, as far as anyone can tell."

"And Victor fell for you—he must *like* girls that are fun, right?"

I sighed. "Or ones who set things on fire."

I scratched and Emma pulled the white ball out of the pocket and addressed me in what I recognized as her Lecture Stance. "Cathy, do you remember what Jun said, the first time the two of you met?"

Was it only six months ago? I tried to remember the conversation. "I wanted to stop at a stream, and she said we didn't have time, and I said we were going to make time because no way was I going to go to my death with barf on my shirt."

Emma laughed. "See, you *are* funny. I meant the other part." She looked over to make sure Jun and Victor weren't listening. Denny was, but he was pretending not to. "She asked which flowers you liked best, fresh ones or fake. Ancestor Lu felt something for Little Sister, the mortal kid, he never did for his immortal daughter."

I thought it over. "So what you're saying is, right now Victor will like me best, and we can live happily ever after until my boobs and my belly button start to meet in the middle—"

"Cathy!"

"—Which is when he will remember that Love is a many-splendored thing, but a butt like a volleyball is a joy forever." Jun had actually missed a shot, for once. Victor walked by her, smiling. "All she has to do is wait."

*

Emma and I were finally on to our second game, Emma having managed to scratch on the eight ball to bring the first one to a merciful end. Over at the next table, Victor blew absently over the top of his empty bottle, making a low, lonesome sound as he had months before when we were sitting together in the darkness of Tirehenge. But this time it was beer, not pop, he had been drinking steadily, and it was Jun he was talking to instead of me. "Do you think sex is better when you're mortal?"

That got our collective attention. Even Denny's head swiveled around.

"Can you even remember what it was like?" Victor asked. "Before, I mean?" He blew another note on the bottle. Jun looked like she had just found a rat in her soup and didn't say anything. "I can't remember for sure, but I think it was better before I 'died' and turned into a . . . monster. This immortal, unnatural, inhuman thing."

Emma put her head down over a shot. "Why is he drinking beer?" she whispered.

"As opposed to rubbing it on his body?" I asked. "Or shoving it up his—"

"Cathy, my point is, with Victor's constitution, he should be metabolizing the alcohol instantly."

"Meaning . . . he can't get drunk?"

Denny belched. "Poor bastard."

I treated myself to another glimpse at the look on Jun's face and then turned away to hide my grin. "I guess some people can make you want to scream even when they're sober."

"Oh," Emma said suddenly. Her eyes had gone all narrow and she was studying Victor with the sudden directed blast of attention that could drop a charging AP calculus problem in its tracks.

"What?"

"I think I understand something about Victor . . ." She shook her head. "I'd rather not say just now."

*

"I suggest we concentrate on applying the mortality serum to my father," Jun said crisply.

Victor nodded. "Agreed . . . And afterwards," he said, warming to the idea, "I can ask *him* if the sex is better!"

*

Back at the table by the bar, Pete let out a little whoop and pumped his fist, causing Victor to miss his shot.

"Did you beat the Lucky Joy security?" I asked.

"Like a drum!" He peered happily at his screen, jiggling his knees and typing in passwords. "Yo soy muy caliente, muchachas." Somewhere over the intrawebz, the Lucky Joy servers emitted The Bloop of Surrender. "Oh, yes!" Pete murmured. "I am a bad, *bad* man!"

*

"Hang on, Cathy," Emma said, leaning her cue against the pool table a few minutes later. "I've got an idea. I'll be back in a second." She walked briskly over to a vending machine, bought a bottle of pop, and then disappeared into the Ladies' Room. At the same time, Victor headed for the bar to grab another bottle of beer, leaving Jun and me awkwardly together.

I want to say right here that if I'd had more sleep, I truly believe I wouldn't have been quite so pushy with Jun. Even a decent nap in the car probably would have kept me from walking over to Miss Snow Leopard 1628, on a sudden impulse, and saying, "Do you even want him?" way too loudly.

That's my excuse and I'm sticking to it.

I half expected Jun to break my nose with her pool cue, but to my surprise she took the question very seriously. (Okay, that shouldn't have been a surprise. What *didn't* Jun take seriously?) Her eyes turned inward, and I had the feeling her mind was going down an old, old path. "You and I have several things in common," she remarked. "To begin with, our fathers do not love us the way we want."

"Okay, that was unexpected." And at least as painful as a whack from her pool stick would have been.

"For many years I have wondered why my father can never love me as he loves Little Sister. I have come to believe . . ." Trailing off, she reached toward Denny. He flinched, then froze, as she traced the line of a scar across his face with one white finger. There was nothing flirtatious about her. It was a sad touch, almost baffled, like watching a widow pick up something that had belonged to her husband. Desolate. Abandoned. "Desire is a wound like any other," Jun finally said. "I think I must heal too fast. So much of love is being vulnerable. How can a man love what he cannot hurt?"

Her finger left the lines of Denny's face. "Do I want him?" She shrugged, shrinking back inside herself and looking over at Victor, who was exchanging small talk with the bartender. "I am tired of being alone." We saw the flash of Victor's smile as he paid for his beer. "He will never love me," Jun said. "Not as he loves you today. But as the centuries go by, I think to have a person who has shared your life, who can remember your story— that's the only thing that makes you feel real, sometimes. That means more than the momentary flicker of desire."

I glanced at Denny, who shrugged and looked away.

Jun racked up her set of pool balls, getting ready for the next game. Hers was a sad, chilly view, and I didn't quite buy it either. She might fool herself into believing what she said, but here's what I think: no woman, even one who is four hundred years old, can be happy thinking she will never be loved. I'm not saying we're all waiting around for Prince Charming's kiss, not at all: but every woman I know needs to believe, somewhere inside herself, that she can be loved—that she can *inspire* love in someone else, be it man, woman, reptile, or alien as yet undiscovered. That she can deserve it.

But as far as I'm concerned, I thought as Victor threaded his way back through the tables to us, *beautiful four-hundred-year-old ninjas with perfect hair can freakin' wait in line.*

"Well, since you seem to have an awful lot of time on your hands," I said, "why don't you let me take the first turn with Victor, just for the next sixty years or so. Then I'll grow old and die and you can have a go," I added helpfully.

"Waiting," Jun said with distaste, "was not my favorite thing to do, even when I was alive."

"You don't think you're alive?" I asked, curiously.

"Alive?" She shrugged. "Compared to what?"

*

When Emma came back from the bathroom her plastic pop bottle was empty.

"Wow. Thirsty?"

"Actually, I poured the pop down the sink. I just really wanted the bottle." Emma unscrewed the cap and gave me a Serious Look ™. "Cathy, I

want you to give me half of the mortality serum."

"Why?" I said suspiciously. The little perfume bottle felt like the only weapon I had, and I wasn't eager to give it up.

"It's safer if we have two supplies. That way if you lose yours, we have a back-up." I made a Pouty Face. Emma glanced over at the immortals frolicking at the next table. "Listen," she murmured. "We don't really know what Jun is up to, do we? We *think* she's on our side, but what if she and her dad made up? What if she is just waiting for a chance to get the serum back?"

I felt my mouth go dry. "I hadn't even thought of that!"

"Come on." Emma hustled me off to the bathroom and held out her plastic bottle. Reluctantly I dug the crystal peach with its little dram of death out of my purse and gave it to Emma. She took out the stopper and tipped the decanter over, spilling a string of golden drops neatly into the pop bottle with the precision that three years of working with test tubes in AP chemistry will give a girl. She screwed the lid back on her pop bottle and stashed it in her purse.

"Feel better?"

Emma grunted. "Wait until we squirt this up Ancestor Lu's nose. Then I'll feel great."

Widow of Eternity

Glitch (Hour of the Homo Superior)

Jun watched Victor make a shot. "There is the question of what to do with the humans when it comes to fighting."

"We're coming with you," Denny said belligerently.

I bent over my shot. "Denny, we're pretending not to hear them."

"To hell with that. If there's dancing to do with this guy, I need to be in on it."

Jun looked coolly over from the other table. "Your courage is admirable, no doubt, but in actual combat you would be less than useless. You would be a liability."

"I seem to recall Cathy kicked your butt the last time you met," Emma said hotly.

"Um," I said. "Maybe I didn't tell the story right."

"Victor and I are warriors," Jun said. "The rest of you are simply hostages waiting to happen."

*

"Guys," Pete said. He was frowning at his laptop.

*

"You smug, superior *glitch*!" Emma sputtered.

"Glitch?" Denny said, momentarily distracted.

"Rhymes with," I explained. "Emma doesn't like to swear."

"Do you think that's really true?" Victor was looking at Jun with the oddest expression on his face, a strange, lopsided smile I had never seen before. It made him look younger. "Do you think only an immortal has any business taking on your father?"

"It's not my intention to offend," Jun said. "I merely state facts."

"I wonder . . . ." Victor blew absently over the top of his bottle. "Take Cathy, for instance. Cathy has been too much for several immortals to handle. Certainly more than I could manage." Victor's tone was unexpectedly gentle. Loving, even.

82.

Emma was watching him like a hawk. I reminded myself to ask her what she had figured out about him as soon as we got a private moment.

Jun shrugged. "Perhaps Cathy is special. I can't see it, but I could be wrong. As for the rest of the mortals . . ." She reached out with her pool cue and rapped lightly on Denny's cast. "I think we know how much use they would be."

"Guys!" Pete said, more urgently this time. "I just got into one of the voice mail systems at Lucky Joy Cleaners. They have their messages automatically converted to mp3 format."

The hair on the back of my neck was beginning to prickle. "Pete, could we skip the technical details and cut to the chase?"

"I've been listening in on their phone calls." He hesitated. "They think they have you surrounded. And they're moving in for the kill."

Mistaken Identity (Hour of the Entry Level Assassins)

Denny grabbed a pool cue in his good hand and hefted it like a weapon he had used before. Jun's hand went to the handle of the knife hidden in her sleeve. Victor froze, staring at the empty beer bottle in his hand. "Oh, damn it." Emma darted over to the table to stare over Pete's shoulder at the screen of his laptop.

"It's weird." Pete frowned. "They *say* they've got Cathy surrounded, but the field team seems to be in San Francisco."

I stared at him. "San Francisco?"

"Yeah." He plugged an address into a mapping program and a cross section of the city came up. "Looks like it's somewhere in the Mission district."

"Maybe I'm just low on sleep," I said, "but I seem to be here. Are those guys just really confused?"

"Maybe these are, like, minimum wage killers," Denny said. "Entry level dudes."

83.

"It's some place called the Celebrity Hotel," Pete said. "They say a clerk at a local store confirmed the driver's license. 'He made the girl show it when she tried to buy cigarettes.'" He looked up, mystified. "It can't be you, Cathy."

"Oh. My God." I swung around to Denny. "It isn't me, but it is my driver's license."

The color drained from his face. "Jewel?" he said. "But . . . you said she was in Texas!"

My mouth went dry.

"She lied," Emma said tartly. "Jewel does that a lot."

I should have said something, but I didn't. Denny closed his eyes. "They're going to kill my sister."

Driven

Except for the faint ugly smell of distant fires it was a lovely day in the parking lot of the Sticks & Stones, warm and sunny and nice, as if nobody was about to be murdered. Jun strode quickly to her car, a black Jag as sleek and glossy and expensive as her long black hair. Emma ran for Pete's big hybrid pickup truck. "I've already got the directions in my phone," she said, "Pete and I will go first, you guys follow us. Cathy, if you get lost, call me!"

Denny lumbered to the battered Mustang, holding his broken left arm close to his chest. It must have hurt like hell but his face was grim and intent, as if pain wasn't important enough to register. I followed him and Victor watched us go. For a moment I thought he would come with us, but then Jun called to him and he turned to get into the Jag. *So be it. They deserve each other.*

Denny pulled open the door on the driver's side of the Mustang, swearing at the jerk on his arm. "I can drive," I offered.

"No."

"My arm isn't smashed up, and I can go plenty fast," I said. "I failed my driving test for speeding, twice. I promise."

Denny didn't bother to answer. He pulled the Mustang's key out of his pocket and jammed it into the ignition. I ran around and threw myself in the passenger side. "Denny, we can't go any faster than Pete and Emma. We don't even know where we're going." No response. I started to lean across Denny to help drag the seatbelt across his poor mangled arm.

"Don't," he said. He backed up fast, swinging the Mustang out of its parking space. Pete peeled out of the Sticks & Stones lot and headed for the freeway, driving fast. We followed.

"I'm sorry," I said.

Denny fixed the rear view mirror. "I know."

"I can't imagine how you must feel, but—"

"Cathy?"

"Yes?"

We passed the site of another grass fire by the entrance onto the freeway. Black grass, scorched and stinking. "You don't have any brothers or sisters, right?"

"Right."

"So shut up," Denny said.

The Mission

We left the sun behind in San Jose. The Mission sky was grey as old newspapers, and the day was chilly, with a fitful wind that sent plastic bags and Styrofoam coffee cups scudding through the streets. The Mission has a reputation for being arty and bohemian, but to me it always looks sad— block after block of three-story walk-ups without yards or trees, just grey featureless tenements and concrete sidewalks with garbage in the gutters— potato chip bags and beer cans and the occasional used syringe—left there by someone who came to San Francisco for a Summer of Love and didn't get out before the Winter of Despair closed in.

"I hate this city," Denny said.

"When the Valley gets hot, the rising air pulls cold water off the ocean

over San Francisco," I babbled. As if Denny cared. "Hot day inland means cold and foggy in the city."

"Do you think she's dead?"

I didn't know what to say.

Pete pulled into a public parking lot half a block from the Celebrity Hotel. We followed after him, with Jun right on our tail. Denny parked the car and ran for the hotel. Victor caught up with him. They looked like soldiers, I thought. Not the parade ground kind, arms back and chests out, but real soldiers—two men heading to a fight where people were going to die.

Emma stayed behind to pay for parking while the rest of us ran after Victor and Denny. We caught up to them standing on the sidewalk outside the hotel lobby. "No sign of cops," Victor said.

"Not yet."

"Jun and I will go up that way." Victor pointed at a fire escape that ran down the side of the building, ending ten feet above an alley. Victor could probably get up to it, and Jun too—she was quick as a leopard, strong and agile. No way in hell was stocky, bruised, very human Denny swarming up there. "I guess I'll just go in the front door," he said.

Victor nodded. "Pete, what was the room number?"

"402." Pete looked much younger than the other two guys—tense and worried.

"They still talking on the channel you hacked?"

Pete flicked a glance at Denny and shook his head.

Emma came running up behind us, stuffing parking stubs into her purse. "What's the plan?"

Denny pushed open the front door. "Get to her room and kill any son of a bitch standing."

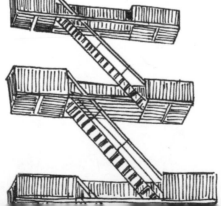

The Celebrity Hotel (Where All Our Guests Are Celebrities)

The lobby of the Celebrity Hotel was dim and depressing. It was decorated in Contemporary Flophouse: dingy light leaking from not quite enough lamps in red shades that hadn't been dusted in the current millennium, and a threadbare red carpet, probably chosen as the answer to the question, "What's the cheapest floor covering you can buy that won't show beer and bloodstains?" Dotted around the walls were three or four pictures of TV actors from the 1970s and 1980s, each picture framed and signed with silver glitter pen. The prize of the collection hung right behind the check-in counter, a bald guy in a trench coat with a lollipop. The inscription said, "Great siopao! Who loves ya, baby?"

Behind the counter was an elderly Filipino whose name tag read "Vicente." He was working the Sudoku puzzle in the daily paper, and the pair of reading glasses perched on his nose gave him a studious look. The bones in his face were very fine and his skin was a warm golden brown, creased into tiny parchment-wrinkles at the corners of his drooping brown eyes. He glanced up at the picture of the old TV actor with the lollipop. "I had a restaurant," he explained. "In Universal City. All the stars used to eat there."

"My sister's staying here," Denny said. "I need to see her."

"Then the economy got so bad, you know. It's a tough business," Vicente sighed, "the restaurant business."

Nothing about the Celebrity Hotel acknowledged the computer age. Instead of plastic cards, the keys were the old-fashioned metal kind, hanging on a Peg-Board behind the counter; instead of a computer screen, the old man reached for an old-fashioned ledger with entries neatly kept in pencil. "What room was your sister in?"

"402," I said. "She's staying under the name of Vickers. Cathy Vickers."

"Does she know you're coming?"

"Sure," I lied. "She called and said we should drop by."

"Mm." The old man found the entry in his ledger. His eyes narrowed. "Do Not Disturb," he said slowly, showing us the words in the Comments

column of his book. He studied me, tilting his head slowly to one side with the expression of an elderly tortoise inspecting a piece of lettuce that was not quite right. "At the Celebrity Hotel, all our guests are celebrities. She said she wanted privacy. Why should I let you in?"

"Um," I said. "Well . . ."

"Because my sister's in trouble, and if you don't give me the key I'm going to kick down the door to room 402," Denny said. "And won't that be a pain in the ass?"

Vicente looked wounded. "Everyone's a star at the Celebrity Hotel," he said reproachfully, reaching for the key on the Peg-Board behind the counter.

Denny grabbed the key and ran for the elevator. "Sorry!" Emma said, patting Vicente apologetically on the arm, but like a tortoise pulling its head back into its shell, he retreated behind his newspaper without another word.

The Lady Vanishes (Hour of the Evil Twin)

Two minutes later Emma, Pete, Denny and I were in the hallway outside room 402. Visions of Jewel danced in my head—Jewel slumped with a broken neck in the bathtub or lying blue and lifeless under a pillow on the bed. Jewel stretched out on the floor like Tsao, with her blood seeping into the dirty red carpet.

"Jewel!" Denny shouted. "Jewel, are you okay?" His hand was shaking so badly he couldn't shove the key into the door lock. "God damn it!"

"Denny." I grabbed the key and opened the door for him.

Jewel's room was a mess, tiny and depressing. A hamburger wrapper and a few French fries were scattered on the unmade bed, along with a newspaper that looked as if it had been pulled out of a trash can, open to the TV listings. The TV was playing cartoons with the sound off. It was so old it didn't have a remote. On the far side of the room a window stood open with its curtain twitching and fluttering in the chilly breeze. Victor and Jun had already found their way into Room 402 from the fire escape. Victor was crouched on the floor, looking under the bed.

"Jewel?" Denny said.

"Nope." Victor got to his feet. "She was here once, but she's gone now."

"Did she leave on her own, or did somebody take her?"

"Hard to say. Look around."

Jewel's purse—a Prada knock-off bought with Tsao's money sometime in the last couple of weeks—lay on the bedside table next to a little reading lamp. If the management had ever supplied even a clock radio, it had long since been stolen. The bathroom was so small that if you sat on the toilet your knees would touch the far wall.

Emma surveyed the room carefully. "I don't see signs of a struggle."

"Maybe she went out for a walk?" Pete said.

I shook my head. "She wouldn't leave her purse."

Denny nodded. "She was always tight with her stuff. Scared someone was going to steal it. I used to tease her about that. There's this Bible verse, we got it in juvie—*the wicked man fleeth where none pursueth*."

"Yeah," Pete said unhappily, "but it ain't paranoia if someone's really out to get you."

I picked up Jewel's purse, as if by touching it I could somehow feel what she was feeling, or see what she was seeing. From the minute she walked into my life Jewel had been nothing but trouble, but right then, watching Denny rooting desperately through Room 402 in search of any kind of clue, I would have given everything I had to see my Evil Twin safe and alive.

the wicked man fleeth where none pursueth.
May Your Enemies Run from You in Fear

"We should call the police." Emma's suggestion, of course.

"Great idea." Victor was flat on the floor, looking under the bed. "More dead cops is just what we need."

Emma pursed her mouth. "I never did like you."

Jun returned from the tiny bathroom. "Victor is right. If my father's agents have Denny's sister, she is beyond the help of the police."

"There must be *something* we can do," Emma said mutinously.

"It's life Cathy, but not as we know it."

Taking Jewel's purse, I walked over to the little bedside table. "Pete, can you still listen in on the Bad Guys chatter?"

"Not here. No WiFi."

"Haven't you got your laptop configured to use your phone as a modem?" Emma said, momentarily distracted.

"I had that hack on my old phone, but when I was installing—"

"GUYS!" I said. "Enough nerdspeak, already."

"It's not like we were talking in Klingon," Emma said huffily.

Victor's head appeared above the level of the bed. "You guys speak Klingon?"

"*HIja'*" Pete said. "*ghIj qet jaghmeyjaj*" He grinned. "*May your enemies run from you in fear.*"

"Dude, even your friends are backing slowly to the edge of the room," Victor said.

"Focus!" I said. "We need to know what the Lucky Joy folks are up to."

The only things on the bedside table other than a reading lamp was an old taco box from a fast food restaurant and a book of paper matches. In my mind's eye, I could clearly see Jewel stepping out the window onto the fire escape for a smoke. I tucked the book of matches in my purse.

Emma punched a series of instructions into her phone and studied its screen. "Okay, there's a coffee shop with Wi-Fi just around the corner. God bless San Francisco. Coming, Pete?"

"Right with ya, boss."

The two of them headed out in search of better browsing. Victor and Jun clattered down the fire escape looking for any sign Jewel had gone up or down it. I grabbed Jewel's imitation Prada bag and started spreading its contents out on the dresser, hoping to find some clue about where she might have gone. I felt Denny hovering at my shoulder. The top of Jewel's purse was crammed with schedules—Metro. BART. Greyhound.

"She used to love maps," Denny said. "Always dreaming of the big trips she was going to make. I would be trying to figure out how to get out to the Gulf Coast for work, maybe pick up a refinery job in Deer Park or Port Arthur; she'd be talking about how we were gonna go to Paris or Prague or

. . . Budapest, that was it. Always said she would take me to Budapest, when she hit it big."

She used to love maps. Already in the past tense.

We spread Jewel's bric-a-brac out on the dresser. Faint shadows of color flickered across it as brightly colored cartoon characters chased and fought each other across the screen of the TV. Outside on the fire escape, Victor and Jun were talking intently, a hushed, urgent conversation.

"Movie ticket," Denny reaching back into the purse. "Hair brush."

"Spare change, chewing gum, bobby pins." Also makeup, a mix of very cheap and incredibly expensive, bought during Jewel's time as Tsao's . . . mistress? Dog? She had turned out to be a dangerous pet, I thought, seeing him again in my mind's eye. He had meant to kill her, but instead he was the one who ended up choking out his life's blood on the expensive carpet in his hotel room. The one thing you could say about Jewel, she was a survivor.

Victor ducked under the bottom of the open window and let himself back into the room from the fire escape. "Denny, come help me scan the hallway and the elevators. If they took her out by force, there's got to be some kind of sign." Denny nodded and followed Victor as if grateful to be out of the squalid little room with its litter of garbage and memories.

My Rival (Hour of the Greener Grass)

As soon as the door closed behind the men, Jun let herself back into the room. She held up a Chinese coin with a hole through the middle. "We found this in the alley."

My heart jumped. "They were here. They came up the fire escape."

"A drunk in the alley remembers seeing a van from the Eight Ancestors restaurant pull up about an hour ago."

"The Eight Ancestors is the first place I ever met Ancestor Lu!" I remembered our meeting. Silence had swept over the people there like a cloud as time slowed and finally stopped; Ancestor Lu an ancient man with a three-pronged beard who had looked at me with eyes deeper than the night sky.

"My father owns that restaurant. I think he is holding Jewel in the Cold Storage room there. He has done things like this before." Jun dropped her eyes and looked away. "It is shameful to have to say these things."

It's not as tough as being kidnapped and thrown into a meat locker, I wanted to say, but I bit my tongue. "Okay, let's go get the guys and get over there."

"No." Jun put her hand on my shoulder and I felt time slow around me, as if I were encased in glass. "If you and Denny go, you will die. Victor wants you to stay here." She let go of my shoulder. "He and I will go."

"So Denny and I are supposed to let you guys do all the heavy lifting while we score a couple of milkshakes at the Dairy Queen?"

Jun pulled the curtain to one side and looked out at the cold grey city outside.

"Three hours ago you were trying to disappear to keep your friends safe. Why would you put them in harm's way now?"

I wanted very badly to break something. I leaned over on the dresser, swore, and slammed my fist on it.

"Are you damaged?" Jun said.

"Hand. Pride. I'll live." I picked through the contents of Jewel's purse, the cheap makeup, the lipstick and mascara and rouge. Eyebrow pencils and eye shadow—the one set of art supplies every girl was supposed to master. All of us building faces against time, pretty as sandcastles, but the tide of years always coming in, coming in, coming in.

"I have to go," Jun said. She paused at the door. "If it makes you feel any better, Cathy, for centuries I have longed to grow old and die like all of you."

"I have to admit, I think of that as more of a bug than a feature."

Jun allowed herself a rare smile. "You know what they say: the grass is always greener on the other side of the grave."

Coyote Never Wins (Hour of Desperation and Loss)

Twenty minutes later, only Denny and I were left in the squalid little hotel room. Denny was sitting on the end of the bed in front of the *Bugs Bunny/Roadrunner* cartoon marathon playing on the TV. Wile E. Coyote was trapped as always in his own personal sand-colored circle of hell, doomed for all eternity to be run over by trucks, shot out of catapults, blown up by high explosives, or dropped endlessly over cliffs three times the height of the Grand Canyon. Denny wasn't seeing any of it. His eyes were locked in a thousand mile stare, surveying his own personal hell, I figured, one with no desert rocks or roadrunners in it: a landscape of pills and broken bottles, his mom and her latest date giggling over dime bags of pot, mustard sandwiches for lunch, and always—always—looking for Jewel. Pulling Jewel out of liquor cabinets, bar fights, or the bedrooms of sleazy thirty-two-year old men, the kind who drive slowly by the local high school between sales calls.

With his bruised face and his arm in a sling he sat on the end of the bed, broken, like a piece of junk thrown out a car window that skids and rolls along the road until it stops for good. He looked like he might never move again.

I hadn't slept in more than thirty hours but I was just the opposite, twitchy and pacing, unable to stay still, unable to stop talking. "God, I hate that Road Runner," I said, stalking around the room. "Didn't you always secretly hope the Coyote would catch him, just once?" I felt thin-skinned, almost feverish, jangly, and hyper-alert. "Like he's standing there and he goes *BEEP BEEP!* and sticks out his tongue and then **snap!** He's got a rat-trap or something and then next thing you know he's eating Chicken Fried Road Runner and wearing his beak on a string as a souvenir."

Denny didn't answer.

On the TV screen, the Coyote went over another cliff, followed by an anvil, a boulder, a grand piano, and a bundle of dynamite. "Story of my life," I muttered.

Denny's crew cut was starting to grow out, blond spiky fuzz on the top of his head. If I ran my hand over his scalp it would feel like cat fur against my palm. When you paint or draw, you train yourself to touch things with your eyes, to feel the nap of a woman's velvet dress or the wet grainy crunch of sand on a beach just by looking at them. Exhausted but wired, it was as if I everything I saw was touching my skin—the itchy white slither of the cheap sheets on Jewel's abandoned bed, the cold greasiness of her leftover fries. I thought about the coarse stubble starting to shadow Denny's face and how I would draw that—the press of the pencil-tip pushing into white paper. "Listen," I said. "I should have told you. Victor and Jun were going to get your sister."

No response.

I prowled the seven steps it took to cross the room from the door to the window, back and forth, back and forth. "The way she said it at the time, it made sense for us to stay, like why should I get Pete and Emma in trouble again, and for god's sake you? I mean, I'm like seven years bad luck for you, I'm a Black Widow. You just show up looking for your sister and I squirt you in the eyes with mouth freshener, and then Victor beats you up, and then I get us caught at a funeral and Tsao breaks your poor arm!"

"Yep," Denny said, voice flat. "I am one tough hombre. Do you think there's any chance Jewel might be alive?"

"But obviously I should have told you. I should have given you the chance to argue with them."

"Jewel might have been out of the room when the bad guys showed up," Denny said. "I didn't see signs of a struggle, and you know she would have fought like a hellcat." I didn't mention the broken necklace and the Chinese coin in the alley below the fire escape. "She might have been out getting breakfast. Or a pack of cigarettes."

"We could go to the Eight Ancestors." I pulled open the drawers in the dresser, looking for a phone book so I could look up the address. "Downtown San Francisco isn't really that big. We could walk there, I bet."

On the TV screen, a big cartoon truck was barreling down the highway and Wile E. Coyote had just realized his feet were glued to the blacktop. Denny grunted and let himself lie back on the bed. "She liked to run the TV all the time. For company." Denny stared at the ceiling. "She hated to be alone."

I found a phone book and flipped through the yellow pages to the restaurant listings. "If we get to the restaurant we can at least be backup for Victor and Jun."

Denny turned his head irritably. "It's not safe. These are honest-to-god killers and in case you hadn't notice, you and I don't have any superpowers."

"Well then, you can stay here and mope," I said, leaning over the bed where he lay to grab my purse. "I'm going to—"

But suddenly Denny's good right hand was wrapped in the collar of my shirt. He jerked me down so my face was inches from his. *"You can't just do what you want."*

He pinned me there with furious strength. I tried to pull away, but all that did was tear out the top button of my shirt. "Let go of me!"

"You think you can just go charging into things," Denny grated out. "One scheme after another. You think you're golden, you think you're like the cat that always lands on its feet, but you *aren't*. Okay?" Our faces were two inches apart but his eyes were frighteningly empty, as if he wasn't even seeing me.

I stopped jerking backwards and tried to keep my voice calm. "Denny? Hey, it's just me, Cathy, okay?"

"I'm the guy that has to bail you out, every single time. And one of these days, I'm not gonna get there soon enough." His hand tightened in my shirt, making it hard to breathe. The thick muscles in his forearm were bunched and trembling with rage and fear. "And I can't let you die. Not after everything. Because if you're dead, I don't want to live."

"Denny. Denny!" I yelled. My eyes found his and held them. *"I'm not Jewel!"* He stared at me, breathing hard, his fist still wrapped in my shirt, but his eyes slowly lost the scary emptiness. "I'm not her," I said.

"You might as well be." Voice still angry. "You want to rush into some god damn restaurant crawling with Rent-A-Ninjas and get yourself shot up."

"I just want to do *something*," I snapped.

"You think bullets just happen on TV, that's your problem. Back where

I come from, people have guns. They use them. Ever seen a girl shot in the back? I have."

"So now I'm just a spoiled middle-class brat," I snarled. "Is that it?" We were both furious now, so close to one another I could feel the heat off his skin.

"Hey, if the shoe fits. Idiot."

"Thug," I said contemptuously. He looked at his hand, as if he hadn't noticed it was wrapped in my collar. He quickly let go. "You ripped my shirt," I said. The button was missing. I didn't look down to see if the edge of my bra was showing.

"Cathy. Please shut up," he said. Then he bunched the fabric in his hand again and pulled me all the way down to his mouth and we kissed: hard, sad, desperate kisses.

In the Desert

Sometimes, when you kiss, it's as if time stands still. Not this time.

There was nothing infinite about these kisses. Nothing about souls. It was two scared animals huddled together to survive. As if time was a desert, dry as old bones, stretching out into eternity, and each kiss was one thin drop of water; as if skin was the only thing to drink and skin the only thing to drink it with: skin drinking skin in a cheap hotel room, in a dry desert, in a wide bleak world where parents didn't look after their children, whatever the storybooks said, and happily ever after was a only a fairy tale, and I hadn't slept forever and I would never sleep again.

Waking (Hour of the Embarrassing Situation)

I had no idea how long I had been asleep. It could have been two minutes, or a year might have passed, leaving me with hair down to my hips and fingernails you could serve fruit kebabs on. The thing that woke me was the sound of voices coming along the hallway. Pete and Emma, I thought muzzily, gradually assigning names to the voices. The door to Room 402 creaked open, and suddenly the voices stopped as if cut with an ax.

I was completely disoriented—no idea where I was or what was happening. My head was lying on something warm that expanded gently in time with the sound of indrawn breath. The inhale was very loud, and coming from somewhere just above my ear. The top of my head seemed to be cradled in a sort of stubbly hollow, and there was something else, thick and heavy as a tree branch holding me tightly around the back, almost as if—

My eyes flew open. I was lying on Denny's chest. The scratchy fabric beneath my cheek was his sling. The top of my head felt warm because it was cradled in the hollow of his throat, and that heavy thing wrapped around me was his good right arm. I gasped and tried to struggle up to a sitting position but Denny's grip tightened effortlessly around me and I was pinned like a Barbie doll clutched in a sleeping bear's armpit.

"Cathy!" Emma said, shocked. ***Shocked.***

The last traces of sleep drained out of me like blood from a vampire's lunch. "Eep!" This time I shot bolt upright by the simple expedient of pushing as hard as I could on the thing underneath me, which happened to be Denny's broken arm. This arm was protected by a cast, but attached to his recently separated shoulder, which wasn't protected by anything.

"O-A-WOA-OWWWWWWW!" he gurgled. "***Son of a—***"

"Emma!" I squeaked. "Pete! What are you doing here?"

"Don't you think that's *my* line?" Emma said tartly. "Under the circumstances?" The eyes behind those little round glasses could have belonged to the Mother Superior of one of the nastier and more punitive convents.

"Not doing anything!" I said.

"No way," Denny said.

"Scouts honor!"

"Injun swear!"

"Er . . . Cathy?" Pete's face was slowly turning red. "Um, you might want to . . . That is, your shirt's kind of undone at the top."

I laughed—a casual, carefree laugh. "Oh, that? No, it's not *undone*," I said. "It's not like I *undid* it."

"I tore it off," Denny explained helpfully.

In the ensuing silence, Emma and Pete's eyebrows rose steadily and in unison, as if being pulled on the same string.

"No!" I squeaked. "Wait! That's not what he meant! I can explain!"

"Of course you can," Emma said. "And I will be fascinated— *fascinated*—to hear you do it. But right now we have more important things to do. Jun and Victor are walking into a trap."

"What!" I scrambled to my feet.

"It took me a while to get back into their network," Pete said. "I had to do some more packet sniffing at the IP, because—"

"Pete," Emma murmured.

"Right, sorry, nobody cares about the technical details. Long story short, when I got back in the bad guys were setting up an ambush."

"Where? Here?"

"They said something about a 'cold room.' Does that mean anything to you?"

"Oh, my God," I whispered.

"No ambush here, then," Emma remarked. "This room has been plenty hot, as far as I can tell."

My cell phone rang. "Victor's Caller ID," I said, but when I flipped it open I heard Jun's voice on the other end.

"Cathy? My car's in the street in front of the hotel. You'd better come downstairs, fast." She sounded scared. "Victor—there's blood everywhere." There was grief in her voice, and shock, and most of all bewilderment. "I don't understand—Cathy, I think he may be dying!"

What Victor Did (Hour of the Ultimate Sacrifice)

I closed the phone. My heart was banging painfully inside my chest like a piece of machinery that was breaking down. Flying apart. "It's Victor. He's hurt."

"Hurt?" Denny and Pete looked mystified.

Emma didn't. Her lips pressed together into a thin line and she stamped her foot. "I knew it!"

"Knew what, Emma? I don't understand. Jun says he's down in her car covered in blood." I got clumsily off the bed. My limbs were numb but buzzing with lack of sleep, with shock, with . . . I don't know. It was hard to move or think. "I saw him get shot through the heart, once. It didn't even slow him down."

"Let's get down there," Emma said.

"Towels," Denny said. "Grab the washcloths from the bathroom and get 'em wet. If there's blood we're gonna need to mop it up to see what the damage is."

"I guess you've done this before?" Emma said.

"Once or twice."

Mechanically I grabbed my purse. Pete was standing at the sink in the tiny bathroom running warm water onto a couple of beige facecloths. He said something to me but the buzzing in my chest and limbs had moved up to my head and I couldn't understand him. I got into the hallway and lurched into a stiff-legged run. It was as if my whole body had forgotten how to work. As if the buzzing in my head was disorganizing me.

Skip.

Suddenly I was standing in the elevator with the others. Somehow my life was starting to skip like a DVD with a scratch in it, time sticking and jumping. The buzzing in my head was worse and the buzzing swept through my body in waves. *Skip.* I realized Pete had been saying my name, but I couldn't remember hearing it. I said, "No, I'm fine." Victor was hurt. Victor might be dying. "I'm good. We should get downstairs." Pete was carrying his

supply of wet rags. I watched drips of warm water roll down his forearm like droplets of clear blood. *Skip.*

We were crossing through the lobby of the Celebrity Hotel. The old Filipino behind the desk was working a crossword puzzle, looking studiously down through his pair of reading glasses. I couldn't remember the elevator doors opening. Instead I had a flashback, not with my eyes but my skin, my whole body remembering what it felt like to be lying with Denny in the squalid bed upstairs while *skip*

Victor was *skip*

while *skip* Victor was *skip*

The humming inside my body was very loud.

Skip. Flash of the hotel door opening, grey sky grey street, cold wind *Skip.*

I was crouching in the back seat of Jun's car. The numb, buzzing feeling broke like a pane of glass and I was completely present. Victor was slumped across the seat wincing in pain and grinning at me in the strangest way. I was trying to run my fingers through his hair. It was sticky with blood. There was blood on his face, too, streams of it. Some thin and liquid, some beginning to get sticky or scabby. A fat ribbon of blood crawled from his clotted hair down his face to his mouth. He licked his lips and it was as if I could taste the blood. "Hey gorgeous," he said. His crazy grin faded and he reached clumsily for my face. "Hey, there. Don't cry."

"I don't understand." Jun was twisted around in the front seat, staring at Victor. "They were waiting for us, but that was always a possibility. It shouldn't have mattered, but they had guns and Victor was so *slow.*"

The backseat door on the other side of Victor opened. Denny leaned in and squeezed one of the wet rags over Victor's head, so thin red blood came rushing out everywhere. "Sucks for your upholstery," he grunted, "but we gotta see what's going on here. Hey, Kung Fu, did you see any sign of my sister at all?"

Victor started to shake his head and then froze as a blast of pain reminded him not to do that. "Sorry," he whispered.

"No sweat, buddy." The beige hotel washcloth was splotched with red as Denny patted around Victor's head. "Un-hunh. Bullet clipped him. You can see the little furrow there."

"Is he going to live?" Jun said that. It should have been me. I could see in Victor's eyes he wanted it to be me, but I couldn't talk.

"Oh, sure. Bullet grazed off the skull. No big deal." Denny dabbed expertly at Victor's scalp and face, lifting the blood off as efficiently as a cop getting fingerprints. "Thing about scalp wounds, though, they bleed like a son of a bitch." I wondered how many times he had done this before. "Might be a little concussed." He held up three fingers. "Hey, Kung Fu, how many?"

Victor stared until he had to squeeze his eyes shut. "*Lots.*"

Denny grunted. "Un-hunh. Listen, dude, I'm guessing you have one hell of a headache, right?" Victor nodded. His face was the color of cigarette ash. "Do you feel like throwing up?" Victor nodded again, wincing. "Well, the lady's upholstery is pretty much shot already, so do what comes naturally," Denny said. "Sometimes you feel better afterwards."

"I'll keep that in mind," Victor whispered. His eyes searched for me again, though he was having trouble focusing. "Cathy? Why are you crying? S'okay, kid."

When I wiped my face it left smear of blood on my cheek. Which was good. I deserved it.

"I don't understand," Jun said, still staring in shock at Victor's pale, bloody face. "This doesn't happen to immortals."

"I know." Emma didn't meet my eyes. "But Victor is not an immortal. Hasn't been one for . . ." She checked her watch. "Three hours or so. Right, Victor?"

He tried to smile. "Guilty, your honor."

"He took the serum!" I whispered.

"Probably while you were getting kicked around in the bathroom at Helga's Pancake Hut. We were all distracted, and you left your purse in the booth right next to him," Emma said. "I started to get suspicious when I saw him drinking at Sticks & Stones—not just drinking, but getting drunk."

"But—" My voice cracked. "But *why*?"

Victor looked at me. Embarrassed. Vulnerable.

"Oh, I remember!" Pete said. "We were in the restaurant, and he said, 'What do I have to do to make you trust me? Drop dead?' and—" Emma gave him a look that made him shut his mouth with a snap.

"And I said, 'It would be a good start,'" I whispered. I looked at Victor, lying battered in the back seat of Jun's car, and a searing pain punched through my heart like an arrow. Like a burning knife.

"So there he was, walking into an ambush, but one hundred percent human for the first time in a hundred years," Emma said quietly.

"Why didn't you tell me!" Jun said. "I never would have let you come to the restaurant!" Victor shrugged and then winced at the pain in his head, and I imagined him walking into the Eight Ancestors having given up everything—*everything*—for me, getting beaten up, risking torture and death . . . all while I was kissing Denny back at the Celebrity Hotel.

Skip.

Everyone was looking at me. Victor was touching my cheek with his shaking hand. His eyes were worried.

"You didn't tell me," I said. "Why didn't you tell me?"

"Didn't want you to feel . . . obliged," he whispered. "Didn't want you to choose me out of pity. Or guilt." He winced. "Christ, my head hurts." There was a lot of blood on his hands and where he touched my cheek it felt sticky. "I just wanted you to . . . to trust me."

Skip.

Cathy (Five Letter Word for Betrayal)

"—him inside." Denny was talking. "Keep him warm. He's looking kinda shocky." I wasn't in the back seat of Jun's car any more. I was standing on the sidewalk. It was cold.

102.

"B'fine, fine," Victor said, slurring the words. "Don't worry about me. Had the crap kicked out of me plenty of times."

"Yeah, well, not recently, buddy." Denny lumbered around to the curbside door, considering. "Somehow we need to get you upstairs to lie down."

"Rest. Ice. Compress. Elevate," Emma said.

"What were you going to compress?" Pete said. "His head?"

"You shoulda seen the other guy," Victor said muzzily. He frowned. "Actually, I wish *I'd* seen the other guy."

"You think the hotel will let us bring him upstairs?" Emma said dubiously. "The manager wasn't keen on letting us in even *before* we were covered in blood."

"Vicente? Don't worry about him," I said brightly. "A little lying will fix us up. That's where I come in!" My voice was starting to veer towards hysteria, sliding around like a drunk on rollerskates, so I snapped my mouth shut.

Denny grunted. "This busted arm is not helping. Pete, help Kung Fu out of the car. Jun, you take the other side. Cathy, you git inside and lay us down some covering fire with the Management."

"Aye, aye, sir." My whole body was humming and shuddering inside, as if an alarm clock in my chest was shaking itself to pieces. I smiled more loudly so nobody else would hear that, turned and trotted into the lobby of the Celebrity Hotel.

Vicente was still doing his crossword puzzle, but he looked up, politely attentive, as I approached the counter. "May I help you?"

"Uh . . . yes! Actually, it's about that crossword puzzle."

His smile became strained. "You want to take my puzzle?"

"No! I mean, I've been working on a puzzle myself, up in the room," I lied. "But now I'm stuck." Out of the corner of my eye, I saw the hotel door swing open. My friends had arranged themselves so Victor had his arm around Jun, as if they were dating. Vicente's eyes drifted over in their direction. Victor's knees wobbled, making him lurch into Jun. A small frown, like a cloud forming, began to shadow Vicente's face. I couldn't let him keep staring at Victor. "I need a word. Adulteress!" I said urgently.

Vicente's eyebrows rose. "I need a five-letter word for 'adulteress'."

Vicente tapped his pencil thoughtfully against his mouth. "Whore?"

"Whore! That might be it!" Victor was halfway across the lobby. "I'm not sure if a 'W' will work for the first letter, though. Can you think of anything else?"

"Cheat?" Vicente said thoughtfully. "Tramp? Bitch? Sleaze?"

"Yes, yes, yes," I said in heartfelt agreement. "Every one of those."

Emma pushed the elevator button, and the doors slid open with a *Bing!* that pulled a groan out of Victor and made his knees buckle.

"Wait!" Vicente said sharply.

Uh-oh. "Please, you don't understand," I said desperately. "It's terribly important—"

"Sleaze has *six* letters." Vicente leaned toward me. "Are you willing to cheat?"

"It looks like it."

He winked. "I have a book." He ducked under the counter as my friends piled Victor into the elevator. "Aha!" Smiling broadly, Vicente resurfaced brandishing *Dr. Doolittle's Crossword Thesaurus*. "Sometimes, you know, for help with my English!" He thumbed through the pages. "Adulteress, five letters . . . aha! Here you are," he said, beaming as the elevator doors slid closed. "'Skank.' 'Hussy.' 'Wench.'"

"Gee," I said. "Thanks."

Victor was safe. All my friends were safe, at least for the moment, and I could keep them that way. Smiling brightly to Vicente one last time, I walked back across the lobby to the front door and headed out into the street. It was cold and the wind pulled at my shirt. I started walking then, moving without purpose or thought or direction, like something you would throw away. Like a piece of trash blowing through the San Francisco streets.

105.

EMP-TY

empty

A ghost with a bloody mouth
Is crying in the Food Court at the mall.
An angel on the subway takes a drag
on his last cigarette
The Devil's in the drugstore buying
Vaseline and Tylenol
It's the things you don't see sometimes,
That you never forget.

(chorus)
A broken doll, an empty house
No handlebars to hold onto
I lost my way, I lost my mind
I lost myself when I lost you

107.

The ghost has been waiting for
The time things would fall apart
The angel's been waiting for the moment
You would leave me alone.

The devil has been whispering
The words that would break my heart
But I got tired of waiting
So I broke it on my own.

(chorus)
I lost the key, and suddenly
There's no home left to go home to
I lost my way, I lost my mind
I lost myself, when I lost you.

Emergency

When I finally came to myself I was looking at an ambulance: the lights flashing blue and red and white, the color of candles on a birthday cake, and the siren like a city's worth of children crying, crying. An old, familiar sound. One of my earliest memories is being three or four, waiting for my mom to get off shift, wandering around outside the glass doors of her hospital and watching the ambulances swirl and fumble around the emergency room doors like bumblebees returning to their hive.

Without thinking my feet turned to follow the ambulance as it turned into a long driveway, and I found myself looking up at the great concrete wings of San Francisco General.

> **Serving 1.5 million residents of the Bay Area.**
> **San Francisco's only public hospital with a level 1 trauma center.**

Another sign announced that they had the only acute care psychiatric emergency ward, too. Lucky me.

I found my eyes were tearing in the mean little wind. I realized I was freezing and I wanted to go inside where it was warm. Instead of walking through the big front doors, I went around the side until I found the emergency room entrance, as if I was a little kid again, waiting for my mom to get off work. SF General had that hospital smell: old linoleum and sick people and the distant odor of formaldehyde. Fluorescent lights hummed overhead. The waiting room had the same sturdy utilitarian chairs they always do, and the same rows of waiting faces, bored and wretched and trying not to make a scene. A sick Latino woman, pale and shuddering with the chills sat next to a working guy with his hand wrapped in strips of white T-shirt splotched with blood. An old Chinese man with a stringy beard sat hunched in the corner, mostly hidden by a potted plant. Closest to the reception desk was a bicycle courier who'd been in an accident, so the right leg of his neon unitard was shredded and mixed with skin and scabbing blood, as if someone had pulled a cheese grater down his leg. He

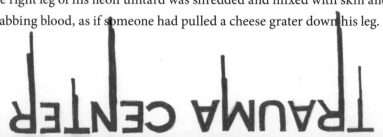

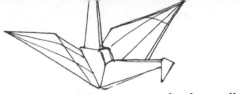

was very careful not to move that leg at all. Broken ankle, maybe, or torn knee ligaments.

The busy nurse behind the glass at the reception desk looked up from her computer screen. "Can I help you?"

I just want to sit here for a while. "I'm waiting for a friend."

She shrugged and I looked for a place to sit down. The other chair by the potted plant was empty. I sat down next to the old Chinese guy, who was making something out of origami. It was Paper Folding Man, one of the Eight immortals. He looked up and our eyes met. "What are you doing here!" I said. "Did you come here looking for me?"

The bit of colored paper buckled and twisted in his old fingers. "Did you?"

Guillermo (Hour of the Good Samaritan)

A young Latino mother, maybe 25, brought her seven-year-old son up to the reception desk. The nurse glanced up. "Which one of you is the patient?"

"Perdon, no hablo inglés. Sorry." The mom was a little plump, wearing discount store jeans and big silver hoop earrings. Her son was skinny, with dark circles under his eyes.

"Que es mal?" the nurse said with a Spanish accent even worse than mine. "You, or him?"

"Guillermo." She rubbed his back gently, and then touched his head. "Aqui."

The nurse mimed a headache and pointed at the kid. Mom nodded. "Sí, sí."

"Okay." The nurse pushed a clipboard across the desk. "Fill out these forms and then turn them back to me." The mom looked at them doubtfully. "Here's a pen," the nurse said.

The mom took the forms and turned around. Paper Folding man glanced at her and looked back down at his work. He was twisting something out of a piece of hell money, folding up the bright colors, making a wing. The mom's eyes darted to me. I smiled at her, and the two of them came to sit beside me. The clock on the wall said it was past three in the afternoon.

The young mother stared at the forms. She filled in the boy's name,

NO.

Guillermo Rodríguez. The place for "date" said mm/dd/yy and she got that, too, although she reversed the order of the day and month, doing it European style. I wondered if she was from Mexico or Spain or somewhere in South America, and how she ended up in San Francisco, and where the father was. I wondered what was wrong with the kid. He was so passive, not like a regular little boy at all. His face was pale and he looked exhausted. I wondered if he just had a regular headache or if it was something worse. I wondered if he was scared. I knew she was.

"Por favor," I said. "Ayudar?" The mom looked at me, confused. Apparently my Spanish sucked even outside of Spanish class. I tapped the forms. "Puedo ayudar?"

"Ah! Sí, por favor."

I helped her fill out the forms. My mom was a health freak who always made me do everything—tests for knee damage, ADD, hearing deficits (I think she was hoping to find some physical reason I always ignored her). I got tetanus shots and inoculations against diseases only found in Cambodian swamps, flu shots and the cervical cancer vaccine and, one time, a tapeworm scan I would rather not talk about. I know my way around a healthcare form better than a lot of people, especially one that isn't in a foreign language. The mother kept apologizing and I kept saying it was all okay while fighting a losing battle with my high school Spanish.

"Guillermo, cabeza," the mom said. "Aqui, he say . . . *como se dice regresar*?" she asked the kid.

"Come back." He leaned his head against his mother's arm. "Come back para el gato."

"Come back for the cat?" The light went on for me. "Ah. CAT scan!" The mother nodded vigorously. I put down the clipboard with the forms. "Let's start from the beginning. De primero," I said. "Guillermo, head, ow. And you already came here." Blank looks. "Aquí," I said, pointing at the room, "but before." I waved back over my shoulder. "Antes."

"Si. Yes," the mother said carefully. She reached into her purse and pulled out a little pink appointment slip for three o'clock in the radiology ward.

III.

Now I understood. The little boy had been sick, or fallen off his bike, or hit his head on the monkey bars at school, and his mom had brought him to emergency, probably because she didn't have health insurance and the ER was the only way she could get a doctor to see her son.

Behind me, paper rustled and whispered under the old immortal's hands.

Guillermo's mother looked at me without speaking. Her eyes were full of passionate intensity. I held out my hand. "Let me take you to radiology," is what I said out loud, but what I meant was *trust me.*

She gave me the tiniest nod, and stood up. "Guillermo," she said crisply. "Vámonos." As we headed for the radiology department, I saw a tiny paper butterfly clinging to the boy's shirt.

*

The kid didn't realize they were going to give him a needle before they did the CT scan. They shoot you up with barium before they put you inside, to help with the imaging. It's a big scary-looking needle but it doesn't hurt or anything, just makes you flushed and sweaty. Twenty minutes after the injection the medical resident shoved Guillermo into the CT like he was putting a fish stick in the microwave. The resident looked like he was about nineteen. He could feel that the nurses despised him but he thought it was because they didn't respect his knowledge, when actually they just wanted him to be nicer to the poor kid.

A CT scan when it's running makes these loud flat cracks, like distant gunfire. The mother stood next to me looking at the med student and saying *Oh my god, Oh my god*, in Spanish. *Oh, my God, he's so young.*

Don't worry, I had said. *No preocupar. This doctor, este medico, he's young, but he's a genius, un genio. Graduated number one in his class*, I said.

El primero? she asked. *De veras?*

Es verdad, I said. *Swear to God.*

*

Paper Folding Man was still there when I got back to the emergency room. His face, wrinkled as an old apple, split into a smile as I sat back down in the chair next to his. "You and me, we *meddle*." He wheezed. "You feel better."

And he was right. I did. It was like I had stopped being Cathy, the star of *The Cathy Show*. I was just some anonymous person who had helped out Guillermo and his mom. I had touched something without wrecking it. It was such a relief to escape from myself for a few minutes. To not be a terrible person, if only for half an hour.

Falling

The time I jumped off the garage and hurt my ankle I remember sitting in the ER thinking how drastically pain simplifies the world. All your usual thoughts—hair, TV, school, whether people like you and whether you want them to—all that goes away. Your world shrinks down to the edge of your skin and it's just you, the animal.

Now, sitting in the ER next to Paper Folding Man, I felt almost the same way; as if my life was a house that had burned down, leaving me on the sidewalk with nothing but the Essential Cathy. I wasn't my dad's favorite girl anymore. I wasn't going to grow up to be a painter like him; thanks to Ancestor Lu, the odds were pretty good that I wasn't going to grow up at all. I wasn't destiny's child anymore, either, the ordinary human who could mix with the immortals and not get hurt. I wasn't Victor's girlfriend; I had thrown that away, and if Emma was still willing to be pals with me it was more than I deserved.

It sounds as if I was depressed, but I had passed through desolation and was in the strange country beyond that. With the burned shell of my old life behind me, I suppose you could say I felt empty, but *stripped down* would be closer; clearheaded, too, and clear-eyed.

All my life, it seemed to me, I had *used* people. Performed for them, charmed and joked and bribed my way into their hearts. Instead of myself,

I gave them *The Cathy Show*, hoping that maybe my thoughtlessness and quick temper and laziness would be forgiven if only the show was funny enough, fast enough.

But the audience had left the theater, and the stage lights were going down. No show left.

Just Cathy.

Self Portrait

This is everything I know for sure:

I jump off things. I also jump over things (sometimes) and into them (often). I have been known to skin my knees.

I wish I didn't care about the way I look, but I care a lot. I like fresh-squeezed orange juice at breakfast and the smell of cooking garlic at dinner. There is a vein of unhappiness in my mother that never goes away. That makes me angry and it makes me feel guilty. I hate that I can't fix it but I know that I can't: and all that being said, it wouldn't kill me to do the dishes a couple more times a week.

I hate waiting and I hate being scared. I've let a lot of people down, but when I can finally stop thinking about myself, I find I still love them, fiercely.

Cats like me.

I can wear orange, which just isn't true for some people, and even when I panic I can usually keep thinking. I'm told that as a child I was very kind to the kids other people made fun of. I don't remember this, but I do know that my teachers always put me at the table with the foreign exchange student. Come to think of it, that's probably how I met Emma.

My name is Cathy Vickers and when I was a little girl I tried to eat a red crayon because it was such a beautiful color. If I close my eyes, I can still remember how it was going to taste.

Learn to Draw (Hour of the Cormorant)

Paper Folding Man reached over and snatched my purse.

"Hey! Put that down!" I grabbed for my purse but the old immortal kept it effortlessly out of my grasp, smirking. He pulled out my Swiss Army knife and my sketch pad, then with little grunts and snuffles dug around in my spare makeup and art supplies. Finally, like a magician pulling a rabbit out of a hat, he held up my purse and fished out the book of paper matches I'd found on Jewel's bedside table. He flipped the cover open.

On the inside was one of those *Learn to Draw!* ads, where some shyster promised that **You, Too Could Have a Career as a Professional Artist!** Jewel had written the word CORMORANT over the ad in block capitals and underlined it three times. I stared at it, mystified.

Cormorant?

Paper Folding Man's nimble fingers pulled out paper matches, two, four, many of them. He folded the matches together, lacing them, his dry old fingers twisting and rattling like twigs in the wind, knotting together a figurine, a little girl in a dress with match-heads for her feet and hands and head.

CORMORANT

Paper Folding Man lit the little match girl's foot. Fire sparked and sputtered into life. When I stepped out into the street in front of the Celebrity Hotel and walked away from my life like a woman leaving a ruined building, it was as if time had stopped. But as soon as the match girl started to burn, it was as if time had started again. There was something urgent about Jewel's matchbook, something terribly important.

CORMORANT. Why would she write that? Jewel wasn't really the type to take notes while watching The Nature Channel.

"You have good eyes," Paper Folding Man said. "Use them!" And fire started crawling up the paper girl's leg, but at last my brain was beginning to wake up and catch fire along with it. What if this matchbook was a message left *specifically for me?*

I tried to imagine what must have happened in Jewel's little room at the Celebrity Hotel.

The TV is on, but Jewel isn't watching it. She is pacing back and forth and looking out the window, because she's a survivor and that's what survivors do, they stay on guard. Jewel is a piece of Lu's dirty laundry. She can feel his need to get rid of her like ants crawling on her skin; she can feel him coming like a storm building on a Texas afternoon.

The paper doll's leg turned black and twisted as flames reached her skirt.

Jewel looks out her window, watching the Eight Ancestors' van pull into the alleyway. From reading my diary, she knows that was the first place I ever met Ancestor Lu. Her Spidey-sense goes off like a high school fire alarm. If she's in this room when Lu's people come through the door, she's a dead woman. She can't go out the fire escape—the van is out there watching for that. She has to play Hide 'N Seek through the floors of the Celebrity Hotel, hiding in the stairwells. She only has seconds to get out of the room . . . but for some reason she grabs her matchbook and writes a message on it, a message meant for me.

CORMORANT.

"A rendezvous, maybe?" I said. "Someplace I can find her?"

The paper doll's legs and waist had burned away, and the matchhead that was her right hand smoked and sizzled into life. Paper Folding Man was watching me intently.

And then I had it. "The cormorant! It was watching the first time I met Victor, down by the seawall on North Beach! And Jewel knows that because *she stole my diary!* She's waiting for me back where this whole thing started!"

Paper Folding Man's old eyes glinted. "Ver' good!" he said, and with a little puff of breath, he blew out the fire on the little paper doll, leaving only her head.

ARTIST

Betray

Parents (Hour of Time to Grow Up)

I had to get down to North Beach. If my hunch was right, Jewel was waiting for me there. Just as I started cramming my sketchbook back into my purse, my phone rang. It was my father. "Cathy! Thank God you're okay!"

A garbled announcement mumbled over the hospital intercom, and I had to speak up. "What do you want, Dad?"

"Where are you?"

"San Francisco General."

"San Francisco General," my dad repeated. I heard voices murmuring behind him. "Is Victor there with you?"

"Who are you talking to?" Paper Folding Man pulled the crystal peach with the mortality serum in it out of my purse. *"Hey, gimme that!"* I hissed. "Sniff that stuff and you'll die!"

"Who's there with you, Cathy? Is it Victor?"

I thought of lunging for the perfume bottle but decided the risk of breaking it was too great. It was the one bargaining chip I had with the immortals. Even though Emma had half of our supply, I didn't dare waste the other half by drizzling it over a potted plant in a hospital waiting room. I glared daggers at Paper Folding Man. He stuck out his tongue—a little pink snake in the middle of his wispy white beard. "Why are you so interested in my ex-boyfriend all of a sudden, Dad? I didn't think you were exactly the chairman of the Victor Chan Fan Club."

"No, I just think we ought to have a conver— did you say *ex*-boyfriend?"

"As of about three hours ago." I held my hand out imperiously. Paper Folding Man scowled but reluctantly gave me back the bottle of mortality serum.

My dad breathed out a sigh of relief. "That makes things easier. Listen, kiddo, some people are on their way over to talk to Victor. I need you to keep him there for ten minutes, sweetie."

My skin went cold. "You're trying to set him up."

"Cathy—"

"You're working for Ancestor Lu!"

"Victor is immortal. You aren't, Cathy. And neither is your mother."

Silence on the line.

"Oh, my God. Dad!"

"Cathy, nothing has happened . . . yet. But, sweetheart, you know how this will go. Lu knows where your mother lives. He can get to her any time he wants."

I had a sudden flash of Mom padding around the kitchen in her slippers, making coffee. A knock on the door. She wouldn't know any better than to answer it. She would pull the door open and—

"No!" I cried. "No! Why! This doesn't have anything to do with her!"

"Lu wants Victor. Victor wants you," my father said. "That's enough,"

"Well, then fix it," I said furiously. "I bet you're standing there with the old psychopath right now, aren't you?"

"Cathy, shut up." My father's voice was flat and dead serious. "This isn't a game. Lu is immortal. He is rich. He is powerful. In cartoons, the underdogs always win. The real world isn't like that," he said urgently. "I need you to grow up, Cathy. This is your mother's life on the line."

"Where are you? Dad? *Where is Ancestor Lu?*"

"They're on their way, Cathy. Just keep Victor there for five more minutes."

I stuffed the mortality serum back in my purse. "I already killed Victor once today."

"What?"

"—twice seems excessive." I stood up and slung my purse over my shoulder. "I'm not turning anybody in, Dad."

"Cathy, your mother—"

"My mother needs someone to protect her. And I can't. But you can." I leaned forward and gave Paper Folding Man a sudden hug. "Dad, if you don't take care of Mom, she's going to die. You have to go to the hospital right now and make sure she's okay." I planted a kiss on Paper Folding Man's wrinkled old cheek and stepped back.

117.

"But, Cathy—" my dad said helplessly, in a tone of voice I will admit sounded familiar. "What do you expect me to say to her?"

"*I'm sorry* seems like a good place to start. I'm going to try it as soon as I get the chance." Paper Folding Man thoughtfully rubbed his cheek and then bowed to me. I bowed back. "Dad, I'm going to hang up now, but if you *are* near Ancestor Lu . . . tell him I'm going to kick his eternal ass."

My name is Cathy Vickers. I hate waiting and I hate being scared, and when in doubt, I jump.

Enter the Dragon (Smoking Menthols, Stage Left)

I started running full tilt for North Beach. After about two blocks, though, my lungs had a short, urgent conversation with my brain. The two of them decided that since it was nearly five miles to where I was going, maybe I had better grab a bus. I ran down to the Embarcadero and caught the F, which plodded slowly along the piers, passing the legions of tourists that mill around San Francisco every summer wondering where the hell the sunny beaches of their California vacation dream have gone in all the dank grey fog. Then it was my stop, and I was sprinting down Beach Street to the part of the seawall where I had first met Victor months ago. I started trotting along the wall, looking for Jewel. My legs felt like lead, I had a stitch as if an angry whaler had thrown a harpoon through my side, and my lungs had apparently shrunk down to two thimble-sized plastic bags that couldn't oxygenate a sleeping lemur.

Even before I saw Jewel, I saw the smoke from her cigarette drifting up from a staircase leading from the seawall to the beach. She was sitting with her back to me, like one of the tough girls hanging out on the steps behind the school. She was wearing the colors, too: blue jeans and a leather jacket and black leather ankle boots with fringes. Her hair was still dyed to match mine. When she took the cigarette out of her mouth, the tip burned a line of orange into the grey day. From behind, she looked smaller than I remembered. More vulnerable.

I shambled to the top of the stairs, grabbed the handrail and leaned over, trying to get my breath. "Hey!" I said, because that's a word you can make just by holding your lips in a certain shape while gasping for air.

Jewel turned around. "I was beginning to think you wouldn't show up." A white tank top under the leather jacket completed the tough girl look. If I was on the run from a deadly killer, I guess I would wear whatever made me feel tough, too. "You stole my perfume."

"Not (*gasp*) perfume."

Jewel took a drag on her cigarette. She'd had a lot of practice not admitting things.

"Serum," I gulped. "That's why Tsao (*pant*) was human enough to die."

Jewel gave a quick jerk of her shoulders, that '*what's it to ya?*' shrug. "Whatever. Point is, I need that stuff to whack Lu."

I shook my head vigorously, because that was a way of saying, "No!" that didn't require any oxygen at all. "*I'm* going to (*pant*) get him. Tell me (*whoop, gurgle*) where he is."

"Damn, Cathy. You're out of breath," Jewel said critically. She took a long drag on her cigarette and let the smoke drift from her nose like a White Trash Dragon. "You need to get in shape." I thought about strangling her, but instead I doubled over with my hands on my knees and wondered whether I could manage to throw up on her. Scratch that: on closer inspection I realized she was wearing a pair of my jeans, stolen during her visit to my house. Ash drifted from the end of her cigarette as she used it to gesture at my shirt. "You got some serious pit stains there."

"Gee," I wheezed. "I had forgotten how much I liked you."

"Everybody likes me," Jewel said drily. "I'm like a cheerleader at a frat party."

I looked up at her from under my sweaty bangs. "Were you ever a cheerleader?"

"I hit one with a beer bottle once. So, where's the rest of the gang?"

I levered myself upright and let the sea breeze cool me down. "I'm leaving them out of the mix this round."

"That Victor sure is sweet. You should have seen some of the purty

things he wrote me!" Jewel drawled. "I should warn you, when we were texting back and forth, him and me, I promised to do some things with him the next time y'all got together. The sort of things nice girls don't do."

Luckily, I was already so red it was impossible for me to blush. "Yeah, well, that's not gonna happen. Me and Victor aren't together anymore." And wanting to make her squirm for once I added, "I got caught making out with your brother."

Jewel froze. "You keep your hands off Denny."

"Come on, now, J, is that fair? *You* don't want to date him, do you? 'Cuz that would be weird."

To my surprise, she grabbed my shirt and jerked me close. I could feel her whole body shaking through her hands. "You leave him alone or I swear to God I will do things to you with this cigarette that doctors cannot fix."

"Jesus!" I shoved her away and the two of us stood glaring at one another. "I'm not hitting on your brother. We were just tired, and he was freaked out because he thought you might be dead."

"I'm hard to kill," Jewel said. That cigarette in one hand and her eyes narrow.

"You might believe that, but Denny sure doesn't." I remembered his face on the drive in from San Jose, when he thought Jewel might have been murdered. "Do you know what your brother sees in me? You. Except a version of you he can save." It was true, I realized, and I could see in her eyes that she knew it. "A version of you that gives a damn about him."

In a low voice she said, "You do not know what we have been through."

"Maybe that's my excuse for how I treat him. What's yours, Jewel?" The stitch in my side was finally easing, and I mostly had my breath back. "Listen, I would love to stand here and chat all day, but I have to go kick Ancestor Lu's ass. I am not giving you the serum, so you might as well tell me where I can find him and be on your way."

A college-age girl on Rollerblades glided around us, followed by a pair of gossiping women with baby strollers and a young stockbroker type talking rapidly into his cell phone in French. A middle-aged dog trotted by, waiting patiently for his middle-aged owner to catch up.

"I have a gun, you know."

"If you gun me down in broad daylight, you're gonna scare the hell out of that nice dog," I said.

Jewel's eyes narrowed to slits. She slung her purse back over her shoulder and took another drag on her cigarette. "Okay, Cathy. As it happens, I do know where Lu is going to be this evening. I'll tell you on two conditions."

"No conditions."

"First condition is, you leave my brother alone." I started to speak but she cut me off. "You like Denny. You should. He's a sweet guy. But you love Victor, and no brother of mine is going to be some bitch's consolation prize."

A black cormorant slid down the ocean breeze and landed heavily on the same rock where he'd been sitting the day I first met Victor. The black bird stretched out his skinny neck and then cocked his head to one side and looked at me through one yellow eye. "Okay," I said. "Deal."

"Second condition." Jewel took another drag off her cigarette. "I'm coming with you."

"I don't like you very much," I said.

Jewel tossed away her cigarette butt. "That's because I do all the things you only wish you could."

"Actually, I think it's because you're really irritating." I picked up her cigarette butt and put it in a trash can. "Okay, you have a deal."

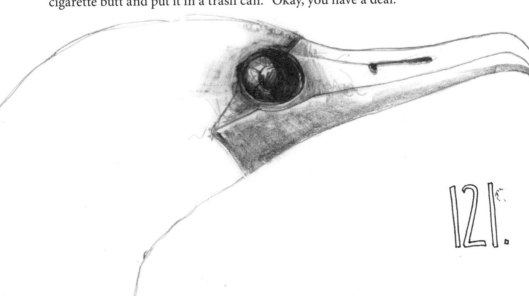

Storm the Castle and Blow Up the Handsome Prince
(Jewel's Bedtime Stories for Wicked Little Girls, Chapter 14 . . .)

According to Jewel, Ancestor Lu was hosting a party for some kid at an art gallery in Golden Gate Park. The kid, of course, would be Lu's mortal daughter, whom I knew only as Little Sister. Lu thought she was the sun and the stars. In a way, she was the real reason for this whole war among the immortals. Ancestor Lu said he wanted everyone to have the gift of eternal life, but the real truth was he was just another father who couldn't bear to think that his daughter would grow up, grow old, and die.

As for the gallery, it had to be the de Young Museum. It was good and it was free; my dad used to take me there all the time.

We caught the N-Judah bus outbound and took it to 9th and Irving. From there we walked into the park. The lack of sleep was catching up to me again. "You look like you're dreaming of snuggling up in your very own cardboard box," Jewel said. "Do you need a cup of coffee?"

"No time," I growled.

"And your hair. Have a little self-respect." She took the cigarette out of her mouth and offered it to me. "You know what they say: it picks you up, and it calms you down."

"I never understood which part of paying money to inhale pollution was supposed to be fun," I said. "Couldn't you just suck on a car exhaust pipe for free?"

"Gosh, you're fun." Jewel put the cigarette back into her mouth. "Come on, Cathy. This should be your kind of thing. This is the part of the story where we storm the castle and blow up the handsome prince!"

"I don't think that's how the story usually goes."

She shrugged. "Yeah, well, real life ain't a fairy tale," she said. "Or hadn't you noticed?"

122.

Little Sister's Circus
(Hour of the Misguided Parental Affection)

Big signs outside the de Young Museum read "Closed—Private Party." Even from a considerable distance away, it was easy to spot the security guards stationed outside the building, neatly dressed men and women with black blazers and headsets. I wondered if they were Lu's personal retinue or if these were Rent-A-Villains, with contracts purchased wholesale from Lucky Joy Cleaners. Jewel's right hand drifted down to nestle inside her purse where her gun was. "Well, here goes nothing," she said.

"Oh, no you don't," I hissed, grabbing her by the elbow before she could start marching up the long path to the front doors. "Do you want to get us killed?"

"Myself, not especially. You?" Jewel shrugged. "I could go either way."

"Well, I have strong feelings on the subject." Reluctantly she let me guide her so we were walking east, parallel to the de Young. "Listen, Jewel, usually being the sane, cautious person isn't my job, so it's kind of freaking me out, okay? But let's see if we can come up with a better plan than playing Bobbing For Bullets with Lu's guards."

Jewel jammed her fists into the pockets of her leather jacket, shoulders hunched against the chilly breeze. "As long as Lu is breathing, you and I are dead as last year's doodlebugs, Cathy. We might as well get it over with fast, one way or the other."

"Yeah, well, I like 'the other way'—the one where we win. What's the deal with that bus, do you think?"

Jewel squinted to read the lettering on the big painted school bus idling in the No Parking zone in front of the museum. "Convent of the Sacred Heart Elementary School. Whoa." She looked at me. "How old did you say Lu's kid is?"

"Ten? Eleven?"

Jewel studied the school bus. "Old enough to be lonely."

"Yeah. I think you've got it. Little Sister's going crazy being locked up at

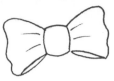

home. Now she wants friends, so he's trying to buy her some."

"Figure he's gonna send her to this fancy private school?"

" . . . And kick it off with a big summer party just before the year starts," I said, nodding, "so all the kids will like her."

We exchanged looks. "So, *that's* gonna go well," Jewel said.

"Poor kid. Can you imagine going to your first day of school with that target on your back?"

Jewel flicked her cigarette butt into the street. "Maybe she's too ignorant to know how bad it's gonna be."

"Will you stop littering?" As for Little Sister, I didn't put much faith in the "too ignorant" theory. I think girls have a built in Suck-o-Meter that would sound the alarm in Little Sister's head the moment the first sixth grade Queen Wasp stepped off the bus ready to crush the newcomer who thought Cool was something you could buy.

We followed Hagiwara Tea Garden Drive and walked to the southeast corner of the museum, then scrambled up a slope to the chain link fence that ran behind the museum. On the other side of the fence was a screen of small trees and a low wall planted with bamboo saplings. A strange assortment of sounds drifted up from the other side of the screen: kids chattering, unsurprisingly, and the clink of plates and glasses, but also old-fashioned horns honking, puffs like a gas fire blazing up and disappearing, and the tinny sound of a merry-go-round with the music not quite right.

Jewel looked at me. "He hired a circus."

Quietly, quietly we slotted our toes into the chain link fence, and quietly, quietly, trying to keep it from shaking or rattling, we inched up until we could just see into the sculpture garden. Inside the compound, knots of fifth-grade girls in Catholic schoolgirl uniforms wandered the grounds, weirdly intermingled with clowns—clowns of all shapes and sizes, at least a dozen of them. There was one clown juggling flaming batons and another one twisting squeaking balloons into improbable animal shapes. Two of them were doing a routine on a teeter-totter and another three were up on a temporary stage. Not far from the stage was a line of tables where

124.

a collection of carnies with white clown skin and scary red clown mouths were laying out place settings of paper plates and plastic cutlery. Another clown was at a serving table, carefully assembling a pyramid of cake slices and stacking plastic cups next to a giant bowl of punch. And, of course, there were big, scary looking clowns with guns standing at the museum doors and patrolling the grounds.

Ancestor Lu sat in the center of the table furthest from the stage. A few yards away from him, painfully alone, sat a skinny, little half-Chinese girl, nervously chewing on her fingernails. Even from across the garden you could tell from her hunched shoulders and downcast eyes that if a meteor were to suddenly come screaming out of the sky and reduce her to something like a bacon stain on a paper towel, it would be a merciful relief.

I caught Jewel's eye and together we lowered ourselves off the fence and far enough down the slope to talk. "Okay, chief," Jewel said. "What's the plan?"

"Mm," I said. The truth is, planning isn't my specialty. Throwing myself headfirst into a cream pie and hoping something good happens is usually more my style. Emma—Emma could plan. Pete was clearly a smart guy. Denny had gotten himself out of a thousand tight places, and as for Victor ...Victor had done it all: soldier, lover, poet, thief.

For a moment I desperately wanted to call on my gang for backup. I so needed Emma and Pete working their Geek Fu, with Jun there to go Matrix on the Lucky Joy thugs. But all my schemes had done for my friends lately was break Denny's arm and Victor's heart, as well as marking the rest of them for execution. For once I was going to have to think for myself.

"Okay, your plan sucks," Jewel said, reaching into her purse. "Let's try the one where we hop the fence, you run up and squirt Lu with the peach juice from hell, and I blow his head off."

"No!" I squeaked. "Terrible plan! Too many guards! We'd never get close enough to him to use the serum. We need a . . . Oh!"

Jewel looked at me suspiciously. "Either a light just went off in your head, or someone stuck a flashlight up your—"

"Disguise!" I said. "We need a disguise, and for once I know just what to do."

125.

Make Up

Ten minutes later we had commandeered the woman's bathroom in the parking garage across the way from the de Young and I was using Jewel's scarlet lipstick to paint a big fat smile on her face. *"Clowns?"* Jewel said disbelievingly.

"Clowns! Now hold still. If you keep trying to peek in the mirror you're going to end up looking like the Joker." I leaned back and surveyed my handiwork. "Not bad. You look even more like a clown than usual."

"Bite me," Jewel growled.

"Next up, whiteface." I rummaged in my purse.

"I'm sure I don't need the whiteface," she complained. "Big red smile, I bet I could already pass for a clown." I turned her head so we could both study her face in the mirror. "Oh my God," she whispered.

"You look like a hooker that lost a fight with a swarm of killer bees," I said crisply. "Sit still and let me work."

"You carry clown makeup in your purse?"

"Aha! Not clown makeup—oil pastels," I said, triumphantly brandishing a stick of white. The clock inside my head kept telling me I needed to work fast, fast. Even someone as oblivious to the world of tween girls as Ancestor Lu was going to figure out the party was a disaster sooner or later and end it before Little Sister threw herself under a tiny pink car with twelve clowns inside.

First I tried to apply the white oil pastel directly to Jewel's skin, but it was immediately obvious there wasn't going to be enough to get good coverage, especially not with two of us to do. Damn. Think, Cathy, think! "Moisturizer," I muttered. I grabbed for my purse and rooted in it like a pig snuffling for her truffle fix.

"I have moisturizer," Jewel volunteered. "I made Tsao buy me stuff in exchange for not actually caring a rat's ass about me." She pulled out a tube of something French and expensive with a price sticker still on it that implied it must have been made from unicorn milk and jasmine flowers pressed at the full moon by left-handed fairies or something.

I took the white pastel and rubbed it furiously on the bathroom counter until I had a thick layer about the diameter of a bagel. "Tsao *did* love me, okay, and personally . . ." I squirted the moisturizer in and mixed them liberally together into a heavy white paste. " . . . I would rather have gotten the skin care products." I scooped up a finger full of paste and slathered it on Jewel's cheek. It looked like I'd slapped her face with a brush of latex paint. "Perfect!"

"When you say 'oil pastels' . . . is this gonna be bad for my complexion?"

"What? Oh, no," I lied. "Besides, it'll come off with nail polish remover."

"*Nail polish remover*?"

"Or turpentine. I'm almost sure turpentine will work."

"*Cathy!*"

Working fast I laid down a good fat coat of white. "Now some expression," I murmured, cocking my head to one side. I grabbed another couple of pastels, green and black this time, and did a few quick lines around my victim's eyes. "Voila! Jewel is gone—and Bobo stands in her place!"

Jewel looked at herself in the mirror. "Whoa. Dude. I'm, like, *terrifying*."

"Clowns are always scary."

"No, seriously, I look like I got mugged by KISS. Little kids are going to cry when they see me."

"Hm." I frowned. "Maybe your Inner Bobo *is* a little scary... here, let me just . . . erase your eyebrows . . . and give you . . . GIANT VULCAN EYEBROWS instead!" The left side of my face twitched as I surveyed my handiwork and I started to giggle uncontrollably.

"Cathy?" Jewel said carefully.

"Yes?"

"Has it been a long time since you had any sleep?"

"Yes, actually. Why do you ask?"

Jewel looked at herself again and shuddered. "Just curious."

I studied my masterpiece, frowning. "Something's missing."

"Nothing is missing," Jewel said quickly.

"Shut up. Artist at work." I stared at her face, leaning in until I was so close her eyes crossed and our noses touched. "A-HA!"

"No!"

"You don't even know what I'm going to say!"

"I know it's going to be horrible."

"Fair point," I admitted. "It's the nose."

"Cathy! Stop!"

Remorselessly. "You *need* a big red nose, Jewel."

"I have a big silver gun already," Jewel said, "and I am not afraid to use it."

I had an idea. "Hang on a sec—I have to go out into the parking garage."

Jewel's big red smile was looking distinctly panicky. "Cathy, what are you going to do to me!"

"And take off your tights while I'm gone!" I called over my shoulder.

I was back in six minutes, panting and gasping, with a pair of antenna balls in my hand. "Wow. There just aren't as many of these as there used to be." The clock in my head going faster and faster, tick, tick, tick . . .

Jewel had dutifully taken off her tights while I was gone, so it was now bare leg that disappeared into her expensive black leather ankle boots. She stared at the antenna balls. "You have completely lost your mind."

"There's a news flash." I dug my Swiss Army knife out of my purse and hollowed out the first antenna ball. "Paint that with the red lipstick, would you?"

"How are we even going to make these stick?"

"Krazy Glue: don't leave home without it."

"Krazy Glue!"

"Relax! I was just joking! Of course we won't use Krazy Glue!" I gave her what was supposed to be a Cheerful Smile but felt a little more like a Psychotic Grin by the time it actually lurched onto my face. "Unless I can't think of anything else."

"I have some sticks of gum in my purse," she said reluctantly.

"That's the spirit!"

Three minutes later she was the proud possessor of one bulbous, red clown nose. The despairing note in her voice was the only thing that ruined the happy jolly clown effect. "Everything smells like spearmint!" she wailed.

128.

"Whine, whine, whine." I scooped up a handful of my improvised Clownface White off the counter and slathered it over myself. "Pass me that red lipstick, would ya?"

"What are the tights for?" Jewel asked, as I gave myself a huge Sad Clown frown.

"Hair. It can't look normal, but I don't have a big red wig, so we have to improvise. Put your hair up and then cut one leg out of your tights to use as a hair net."

"So I'm going as Bobo the Bank Robber?" she said dubiously, pulling the tights over her head.

"No, we can't stop there. You need a hat."

"I don't have a hat."

"Sure you do," I said, pointing to her drawstring purse.

Jewel slowly shook her head at me and began to grin. "You know, sometimes I think there's a kind of crazy genius about you, Cathy Vickers. Except for the genius part." She scooped up her bag and retreated to a cubicle. "Excuse me while I go to the changing room."

"Modest about putting a bag on your head?" I said, mystified.

"No," Jewel said, pulling the gun out of her purse. "But if I'm wearing my bag on my head, I need somewhere else to put this. I figure I can strap it to the inside of my leg."

"Thank God you've got skinny thighs," I said, drawing little blue tears running from my sad clown eyes. It wasn't that funny, but Jewel's laughter bubbled up over the stall doors and made me grin.

By the time she came out of the stall, I was working on my own hair. Jewel had lit another cigarette. "You know those things will kill you," I said absently.

"Ever since I was sixteen, I've had this fantasy about dating the Surgeon General," Jewel said. "Is that perverted?"

"It's the warnings, isn't it?"

Jewel took a drag on her cigarette. "He just seems like a Take Charge kinda guy."

I stared in the mirror. My Sad Clown face was pretty good, but I was

129.

going to have to do something about my hair, and my purse, unfortunately, wouldn't work so great as a hat. "Jewel, can you do braids?"

"Me?"

"Didn't you ever do that? Go over to a girlfriend's house and then you do each other's hair?"

"I guess," Jewel said. "But it's been years and years. Mostly when I sleep over these days, it's with guys."

"Yeah, I figured that out," I said dryly. I turned to face the mirror. "Come on—braid my hair."

Hesitantly, Jewel came up behind me. "Regular braids, or French braids, or . . . ?"

"Quick braids. Whatever you got," I said. "Just go fast!"

Hesitantly she touched my hair. "Are you sure you want me to? It's just . . . usually only friends do that."

"So pretend we're friends," I said impatiently. "Sisters, even." Another wave of exhaustion went through me and for a second I almost remembered about kissing Denny, about the look in Emma's eyes when she found me lying there in the hotel room in his arms. Almost remembered about Victor with blood dripping down his face. Eternal life lost because of me.

I pushed the images away, shook my head and stared into the mirror to see Jewel staring back at me. For some reason her eyes were shiny. "Sisters," she said. "Okay."

*

Hanks of hair like dark ribbon, crossing and recrossing. Braids are like stories, I thought fuzzily: all knotted together, sleek and soft. Like lives.

*

Jewel did my hair in three braids, made them as fast as she could and anchored them with two bobby pins and a rubber band from my purse. Then I got out my useful little bottle of pastel fixative and gave my hair a first spritz to make it sticky. After that we shoved everything we could think

of into those braids: coins and twists of silver foil from Jewel's chewing gum wrappers, then sticks of gum themselves and a couple of lipsticks and an eyebrow pencil and our bus tickets from the ride here and a French fry Jewel had dumped out on the counter when she was emptying her purse. I didn't know Jewel had also plaited half a pack of cigarettes into my back braid until after she had gone over everything with a second coat of fixative, locking them in place.

"Jewel! You put glued cigarettes into my hair! You realize there are kids at this party, right?"

"Hey! These are good smokes I am sacrificing for the cause. Cut me some slack."

"Oh, sure," I said glumly, poking my stiffening hair with one finger. "But I'm the one who gets blamed if this starts a craze for tobacco-themed hair-care products."

"If it happens, honey, I'm just that much closer to a hot date with the Surgeon General," Jewel purred. "*Mrow!*"

At this instant the bathroom door swung open and a plump middle-aged Indian woman in a sari froze in the doorway, staring in at us. Her eyes moved slowly from Jewel's hideous grinning clownface to the counter I had been using as a palette, with pools of white and red pastel-and-moisturizer goop liberally furred with antenna ball fluff, so it looked as if I had been gutting lemurs in the bathroom sink.

A clump of ash fell from Jewel's cigarette and drifted to the tile floor.

I cleared my throat. "So then *I* said, 'Bill, if you make me walk behind the elephant one more time in those white shoes, *I quit!*'"

The nice lady in the sari edged soundlessly backward and the bathroom door swung shut.

132

Double Cross (Hour You Knew Was Coming)

Minutes later we were hiking back up the slope to our spy spot on the edge of the sculpture garden. I paused and unslung my heavy purse, bulked up now by the weight of all of Jewel's assorted junk as well as my own. Carefully I lifted out the little perfume bottle with the mortality serum and put it in the pocket of my jeans. God help me if I were to trip and smash it. My purse I stashed under a tree with a piece of bracken over it for camouflage.

Jewel and I tip-toed to the chain link fence. Jewel touched me on the shoulder. "Me first," she murmured. I shook my head. "Please," she said. Her eyes were serious. "I don't regret what I did to Tsao," she murmured. "He was a snake and he got what was coming to him. But I was the one who dosed the fortune teller, even though I didn't know what would happen. Lu had her killed and that was my fault. I want to make up for that."

I held her eyes, trying to guess if she was sincere, or if she had some scheme she was trying to run and this was more of her usual BS. Maybe both. "Okay," I said at last.

"Thanks." Jewel hooked her fingers in the fence and despite her knee-length skirt, she made her way up like a girl who had broken-and-entered more than a few times. As she swung her legs over the top of the fence I saw a brief glimpse of the gun strapped to the inside of her leg with the half of her pantyhose she hadn't used as a hair net. A moment later she was down on the other side and we were facing each other through the fence, Demon Clown to Sad Clown, with only a bamboo hedge between Jewel and Little Sister's party. "Okay, Cathy, time for you to get out of here," Jewel said. "You get on back to your friends now, and you make sure my brother gets out of this mess, you hear?"

"What? In case you've forgotten, I have the serum," I hissed.

"Not so much." Bending over, Jewel reached into one of her suede boots and pulled out the little tube her expensive moisturizer had been in. "While you were getting antenna balls, I poured the serum out of the perfume bottle."

"What!" I grabbed the perfume bottle out of my pocket and spritzed it against my wrist. No smell of peaches and formaldehyde: just droplets of ordinary tap water. "Damn it, Jewel!"

"Bye-bye doll." She leaned forward briefly until our clown noses bumped. "Thanks for letting me do your hair." Then she turned, slipped through the bamboo hedge, and disappeared into the sculpture garden.

Hour of the Sad Clown

I stood in front of the fence, trying to decide what to do. Common sense said run away. Jewel had the serum and the gun; I was both useless and powerless. Basically, I had two directions I could go: forward into a compound swarming with Ancestor Lu's hired killers and—probably meaner—an army of over-privileged ten-year-old girls. On the other hand, if I turned back I would have to face Emma, Pete, Denny, Victor, and Guilt.

Easy call. Forward, ho!

Hooking my fingers into the chain link fence I went up fast and dropped over the other side, pleased to discover that the mad skillz I had honed over years of ditching gym class were still with me. I could hear clown horns honking and the patter of someone doing a magic show, so Little Sister's party wasn't over yet. I hurried along behind the bamboo hedge, sneaking by a few odd sculptures hidden back here away from the main garden: a striding angel with no arms, a giant distorted head with crosshairs drawn on it, a bronze girl doing a handstand.

My heart was racing as I came around the edge of the bamboo and stepped into the main grounds. The party wasn't over, but it was clearly winding down. Restless fifth-grade girls cruised the grassy expanse of the sculpture garden, sitting on the red metal apples and banging their heels against the Do Not Sit signs, putting various pieces of clothing on the bronze Bean Bag People, or swinging around the Giant Blue Safety Pin. The pyramid of cake slices on the serving table had been reduced to rubble and the big bowl of punch was almost empty. A wreckage of paper plates, chocolate-smeared napkins, and plastic utensils fluttered in the chilly wind as clown-costumed wait-staff went around picking up trash. I spotted Jewel doing clean-up duty, edging slowly toward the Head Table where Little Sister still sat miserably alone. Ancestor Lu was sitting next to her, holding a plastic tumbler of punch and murmuring something in his daughter's ear.

My eyes abruptly refocused about six inches in front of my wrinkling nose as a big hairy clown with powerful BO shoved a balloon cart at me. "You got to cover for me, man," he muttered. "I have SO got to take a leak."

"Gack!" I said, jumping back. "But—"

The hairy clown jerked his thumb at an eager blond girl wearing a nametag that said BRIANNA BERGKAMP. "This one's next."

I gulped. "Hey, Brianna," I said brightly. "Would you like a balloon animal?"

"I want a puppy!" she said enthusiastically.

"I'll give you a snake!" I countered, even more enthusiastically. I stuck a long thin balloon on the nozzle of what I hoped was compressed air. I hit a button and the balloon blew up into a two-foot long pink hot dog. I tied it off and handed it to Brianna, who looked dubiously at it. "Sssss!" I said, weaving my head back and forth so my braids rattled. "S-s-s-lithery s-s-s-snake!"

Brianna's brows furrowed. "But—"

"Next!" I chirped, shoving my balloon cart in the general direction of the head table, where Jewel was now only a few yards away from Ancestor Lu.

A hard-faced, fifth-grade princess named SIERRA came up to me. She was working a designer handbag and skating as close to the Early Britney Teen Slut look as the Sacred Heart Dress Code would allow. "How about you, sweetie?" I cooed. "Would you like a balloon snake?"

"I want a mouse."

"How about a worm?"

"I saw what you did to Brianna. You didn't really make her an animal at all."

My panicked smile and my Sad Clown mouth struggled for control of my face, with doubtless disturbing results. "Or a lovely balloon eel?" I suggested.

Jewel crossed behind Ancestor Lu, carrying a load of garbage to the big plastic cans.

135.

"snail or a slug :

"I don't want an eel," Sierra said, eyes narrowing. "I want a mouse. If you don't make me one, I'm going to talk to your manager."

"Mouse it is!" I promised. "But if you wear that expression too long, honey, it's gonna stick that way. You don't want to go through the rest of your life with Cafeteria Lunch Lady face, do you?" I stuck a red balloon on the nozzle and it blew up into another two-foot long hot-dog shape. I put both hands on the balloon, about three inches apart, and squeezed, making a bulge in the middle. "Here you go, honey bun!"

136. "Where's my mouse?"

"It got eaten by a balloon snake!" And then, loudly, "Next!"

Jewel was returning from dumping her load of trash now, slowing as she came directly behind Ancestor Lu. She bent over as if reaching for a stray paper plate on the ground and slid one hand down into her boot. One of the Security Clowns barked out a warning. Jewel dragged out the tube of moisturizer with the serum inside, but before she could twist off the cap the Security Clown clubbed her to the ground with his gun and then kicked her twice in the stomach, hard.

And just like that it was over. Jewel was lying curled up in the dry grass as Ancestor Lu gently pulled the moisturizer tube out of her hand. Two more Security Clowns ran over with guns drawn to a chorus of excited fifth grade shrieking.

sausage dog?

"*Damn*," I whispered.

"That's *cussing*," Sierra said grimly. "*And* I don't think this is a real balloon mouse. *And* you have *cigarettes* in your hair."

A pair of Killer Klowns dragged Jewel to her feet and started hustling her toward the doors leading into the museum. You could tell she was hurt from the way she lurched between them, hunched and staggering. I had the bad feeling that once she passed into the shadows inside, out of public view, she would never come out of that building alive. I put my head down and pushed the balloon cart ahead, bumping over the dry grass toward Ancestor Lu.

Ancestor Lu put the tube of mortality serum down on the table and turned to watch Jewel get carried away.

maggot

rat
in
snake

Sausa

The serum was lying on the table undefended and Lu's back was to me.

A piping voice announced that the relentless Sierra was still trotting at my side as the Balloon Cart jounced and rattled over the grass. "Have you ever seen a picture of a smoker's *lungs*?"

Now the Killer Klowns were at the museum doors. The coins cemented into my stiff braid bounced against my neck as I hurried over to the picnic tables. Little Sister was staring at her Papa's back. The museum doors swung open . . . and my Dad came through them.

You're supposed to be with Mom! I wanted to scream, but I had to keep quiet and move fast because I was only going to get one chance to grab the moisturizer tube and squirt Lu with the mortality serum inside it. After that . . .

"Do you want to *die*?" Sierra said.

I abandoned the balloon cart and sprinted for Lu's table. Fifteen steps, ten, five more and I would have the serum. If I could just spray Lu with it, at least I would have put a dent in his armor. At least my friends would have a chance.

Everybody was looking at Jewel and away from me: everybody except my father. *Don't see me, don't see me,* I thought, willing him to stare at Jewel like everybody else while I closed the last few precious steps. I lunged past Little Sister and reached for the mortality serum. *Don't see me, Dad, I'm nothing but a Sad Clown to you now.*

But my father has been painting portraits for seven hundred years, and good eyes run in the family. "Cathy!" he shouted. "No!"

I actually had my hand on the serum when Ancestor Lu turned and grabbed my arm. For once, even though I was battling an immortal, time didn't stop for me. For a brief second we tussled for the precious serum. Then Lu had my wrist in some kind of joint lock and I was kneeling in front of the old man with my eyes watering at the pain shooting up my arm.

"Ah. It's Victor's girl, looking like a sad clown." His eyes were black and cold as stones. "How appropriate."

137.

poop

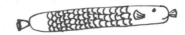

lamb

138.

An Unexpected Party

Ancestor Lu crooked his fingers to summon two more of his Bobo Brigade. "Take this girl somewhere quiet and . . . leave her there."

"*Leave* her there?" Little Sierra, a young lady clearly long on persistence, had followed me right to the head table. Her eyes locked on Little Sister, holding her responsible for what her grown-up was saying. "What does *that* mean?"

"Lu Tung Pin," my father said, keeping his eyes downcast and humble. "Please. We talked about this."

"I will spare your wife," Ancestor Lu said. "She knows nothing. But this one . . ." His old eyes looked at me the way a gardener looks at a weed. "This one has been a trial to me."

"Father," said a clear, cold voice, "I think you must reconsider." Ancestor Lu's grip on my wrist loosened. Looking up, I saw Jun, dressed all in white, standing framed in the museum doors. Her black hair slid and whispered against her white jacket. In her hand she held the ivory-handled knife.

"Jun!" Little Sister cried. A dazzling smile lit the girl's face, and I realized something I hadn't understood before, which was that she loved her big sister and had missed Jun terribly since Lu had exiled her from the house. "Jun, you came to my party!" Little Sister said. "Papa told me you weren't coming, but I knew you would!"

"Ni hao, Little Sister," Jun said softly, and the steel certainty in her eyes when she faced her father faltered.

Then Emma walked out from behind Jun.

*

"Emma!" I stammered. "What are you doing here?"

"Coming to the rescue—" She stopped dead. "Good grief, Cathy! What have you done to your hair!"

Pete appeared behind her, followed by Denny and Victor. The friends I thought I would never see again had risked their lives for me—again. After everything that had happened. They were all there and they were all staring at my giant red mouth, antenna ball nose, and demented magpie braids.

"Whoa," Pete said. "Dude! You look . . ." Speech failed him.

"No lie," Denny said, shaking his head in wonder.

The ghost of a smile crept over Victor's pale face as he beheld the clown-faced splendor that was me. "I think the word you're searching for is . . . *spectacular.*" In truth, Victor didn't look so great himself: determined but very pale, with his eyes half-closed as if even the cloudy San Francisco sky was too bright for him.

There was a knot in my throat the size of a grapefruit. The fact that after everything they would come back for me, that fell on my heart like rain after wildfire season. That felt like forgiveness.

I shrugged and held up one sticky braid, glinting with coins and gum and bits of trash. "They say you never get a second chance to make a first impression." My eyes slid over to Victor. "But I'd sure like to try."

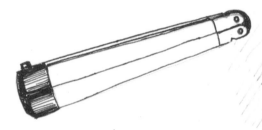

The Bullet

"Talk later," Jun said crisply. "Fight now."

Before anyone else could even blink, her fine black hair spun into a violent blur of motion, and then suddenly the two armed clowns who had been holding Jewel fell to the ground, each clutching what looked like a broken knee. Jewel sagged and started to fall. Denny jumped forward and caught her awkwardly in his one good arm. "Get her inside," Jun said. Denny nodded and pulled his sister back through the doors into the museum.

"Jun, this is not your business," Ancestor Lu said.

Jun stepped forward over the writhing clowns. "The honor of our family is always my business."

Ancestor Lu frowned and turned to my father. "You called Cathy's

friends. You told these people where to find me," he surmised.

My father kept his eyes carefully turned down to the dry grass. "Yes."

"And you helped them past the guards at the museum doors." My father didn't speak. Ancestor Lu shook his head. "These will only be more ghosts at your bedside, Michael Vickers. More deaths for you to repent."

"No, Father." Jun looked around at the assembled clowns and the gaping schoolchildren. "You will dismiss your men and turn Cathy over to me."

"How do you count the odds?" Ancestor Lu said. "According to my reports, Victor has become very . . . delicate." Victor's face was grim and determined, but he was pale and all too clearly not the soldier Ancestor Lu would have seen the last time they met. "As for him . . ." He glanced contemptuously at my father. "I am unlikely to die from a paint brush wound."

"If you're just counting immortals," Emma said, "the score is Two v. Nil, I think."

Ancestor Lu flicked at the tube of serum with one ancient fingernail. "Perhaps you arrived too late to see the show. Cathy failed."

Emma looked steadily at him through her little round glasses. "Maybe, but I didn't."

"You claim to have used the serum on me?" Ancestor Lu laughed. "A bold bluff! And what magical powers did you use to accomplish this miracle? Did you turn invisible, to walk through the garden and poison me as I sat? Or perhaps you made the long climb up the heavenly mountains to T'ien, where you begged an audience with Shang-Ti, the Celestial Emperor, and persuaded him to withdraw the gift of eternal life he gave to me two thousand years before you were born?"

"Nope," Emma said. "I just paid the caterer fifty bucks to dump the rest of the mortality serum in the punch."

Dead silence. The cold wind tugged at red clown wigs and pushed paper napkins across the dry grass.

"Oh," I breathed. "How beautifully, perfectly Emma of you."

Ancestor Lu looked down at the empty plastic cup, then back at my best friend. He swallowed. "You're bluffing."

Quick as a leopard, Jun darted forward. The knife flashed in her hand. An instant later she was standing before her father with her hands folded in front of her and her head respectfully bowed. Ancestor Lu let go of my wrist and stared at his arm, where Jun had cut him, ever so lightly, with her knife. A thin red line of blood welled up just below the elbow, and a single drop trickled down his forearm. A second red bead gathered in the cut, filled like a cherry bud swelling in spring, trembled, and ran after the first.

Then a third drop, and a fourth.

Jun opened her slender fingers and let the knife drop from her hand. Her father wasn't healing. *He wasn't healing.*

Victor sighed. "Someone said once that a gun goes off the moment we are born. It's never a question of *if* the bullet will find us." He nodded at the wet trails of blood creeping like tear-tracks down Ancestor Lu's arm. "Only *when*."

Ancestor Lu turned to his daughter. "You have killed me!" he whispered.

"No," Emma said tartly. "I did."

Crime and Punishment (Hour of the Suddenly Mortal)

Jun barked out a series of orders in Chinese. After a long moment of uncertainty, several of the clowns put their fists against their palms in a Chinese bow and withdrew. The girls from the Convent of the Sacred Heart Elementary School, who had been dead silent from the moment she appeared, began to twitter and buzz, discussing what was obviously going to go down as the best field trip ever. Their chaperones bundled them onto their bus while Little Sister, their classmate-to-be, demanded a first aid kit from a museum employee and fussily applied a Band-Aid to Ancestor Lu's arm.

Victor went into the museum to help Denny with first aid for Jewel. That left me, Emma, Pete, and Jun in a council of war, with my dad standing off to one side. "So what do we do with this guy?" Pete said, jerking his thumb at Lu.

"Leave him to me," Jun said. "I will see he does no more harm."

"Thanks awfully, but that's not enough." Emma's voice had slid into its most British register. You had to know her well to realize that exaggerated

Englishness was a sign of pure rage. "He had Carla Beckman killed. He had the fortune teller killed. He had men casing my apartment and he sent his thugs to murder Cathy. It's not enough."

Jun looked at Emma as a hawk might look at a robin. "Never the less, he is under my protection," she said flatly. "What he did before he was human is not for you to judge, nor any mortal."

Emma's right hand balled into a fist. "Emma!" I rapped out warningly, but Pete was way ahead of me. He grabbed her hand and murmured something into the nape of her neck, looking for all the world like a man trying to calm down a Very Angry Pony, if you can imagine the pony with a sleek black mane and little round glasses.

"Look at Lu. He's an old man now," my father said unexpectedly. And it was true. I had always thought of Lu as ageless, but with his aura of invulnerability gone, he seemed older and more frail, his spine hunched against the unkind wind; as if the tide of time, so long held back, was finally rushing over him with redoubled force. "He won't last long, now."

"Welcome to the world of arthritis," I said.

"And dentures," Pete added.

"Scoliosis. Hip fractures. Incontinence. Senility." Emma named them off like plagues she was calling down.

"Not fun," my dad agreed. "But that isn't the punishment." His eyes subtly indicated Little Sister, who sat curled up beside the old man her father had somehow become. "The real punishment is that he has a beautiful daughter, whom he loves more than life itself . . . and he will never live to see her grow into a young woman. He will never get a chance to know that she is grown-up, and capable, with a strong heart and good friends and a man who loves her." My dad was looking at me. "Nothing you can do will hurt him worse than that."

Cleaning Up (Hour of Reconciliation)

Clean up time. The Lucky Joy flunkies had melted away on orders from Jun, leaving the regular carnies to pack up their equipment. Emma was helping two clowns with wrenches and giant floppy feet to disassemble the teeter-totter and miniature merry-go-round. Since I have roughly the mechanical aptitude of a sea cucumber, I figured wandering around the sculpture garden with a plastic bag picking up loose bits of trash was a better match for my skill set. My dad came over to help and we worked together in awkward silence, picking up plastic cutlery and cake-stained paper plates that the restless wind had pushed all around the sculpture garden.

"I heard about what Victor did," my Dad finally said. "Taking the serum. He must love you very much."

I crumpled up another paper plate and shoved it into my plastic bag. "As God is my witness, I can't see why."

"I can."

Somewhere at the edge of the garden a bird called. The faint smile appeared on my dad's face. "Name that bird, Cathy." A game we had played a thousand times.

I held still and listened until the call came again. "Warbling vireo?" I guessed.

"The girl gets it in one."

The vireo sang the sun down. Twilight was coming on. I said, "It can't ever be like it was, Dad."

"I know."

"Every time I look at Mom, knowing you're alive, it feels like I'm lying to her."

"Do you think I should do what Victor did?" my father asked. "Take the serum. Go back to your mother. Grow old and pass away."

Yes! my heart said. But that was the kid in me talking, the same outraged voice that cries out in every child whose parents get divorced. "Honestly, Dad? I have no idea. I know I don't want you to die." He looked away but I could tell it meant a lot to him that I would say that.

He ran his hand over his receding hairline in a gesture so familiar it made my heart catch. "I don't even know if she would want me back."

I imagined my mother's response to discovering she had been tricked into believing she was a widow. "You might want to keep those super-healing powers until *after* you broke the news," I admitted. That got a laugh out of him.

We walked together side by side. It wasn't like the old days, when I was a kid. Back then we would go out birding together, him toting his easel for doing *plein air* paintings, me trotting along with my sketch book and the special kid-sized binoculars he gave me on my seventh birthday. It couldn't ever be like that again: but it was okay.

Emma (Hour of the BFF)

When the merry-go-round was suitably dismantled, Emma came over to help me roll the balloon cart down to the curb in front of the museum. We stood under the grey sky, not quite making eye contact. I took a deep breath and said, "Emma, I know I owe you an apology—"

"I keep giving you these phones," she said at the same moment, so the two of us were talking over top of one another. "The least you could do is answer my calls—"

"I didn't want you to be in any danger—"

"We got up to the room and nobody knew where you were—"

"After everything I did to you guys—"

"Until your dad called, we thought the Lucky Joy people had kidnapped you—"

"I just . . . I just can't believe you came back for me," I finished.

Emma looked at me. Her habitual businesslike expression slowly dissolved into something entirely different, anguished and afraid. Her shoulders started to shake, her eyes turned wet and shiny. When she had first come to America, back in the eighth grade, she used to do that thing Asian girls do of covering her mouth with her hands when she laughed or cried. She had ruthlessly stamped out that mannerism, trying to fit in, but now her hands flew to her face as she started to weep. "Oh, God, Cathy! Cathy, I thought I'd lost you!" She stood there, the girl who never cried, and her whole slender body was convulsed with sobs.

"Shh! Emma! Emma, it's okay, I promise you. Everything is going to be okay."

"*You're my whole f-family,*" Emma cried. "D-don't you ge-ge-get it?" She was blinking continuously, crying so hard she couldn't catch her breath. "You're the only one I've g-got. You ca-can't just run off on me, C-Cathy!" She grabbed my arms and shook me. "Stop *d-doing* that!"

Gently I tried to give her a hug. She grabbed me like a drowning woman and held on tight. "I am so sorry," I whispered. I was shocked and humbled by the gift of her loyalty. It wasn't as if I had done something to deserve it; that kind of friendship is an offering from the universe, like a beautiful sunset; it's not something you earn, it's an act of grace, and all you can do is be grateful if it happens to you.

Emma was always so smart, so sure of herself and so together that I forget how small she was. Rocking back and forth, locked in our hug, I could feel her little frame shuddering with tears, I thought of all the things I'd put her through and I started bawling, too. There we stood for a good five minutes, hugging each other like a pair of limpets and crying, as if the pressure and fear of the last few days had turned our insides to water and all we could do was wring ourselves out.

Finally Emma loosened her grip. I shuffled back so I could see her tear-stained face. She wiped her wet eyes with the back of her hand. I wiped my runny nose with the sleeve of my shirt. "Emma, I am so sorry."

She reached out and touched one of my stiff-n-sticky braids. "Oh, your poor hair!"

"I guess I should get cleaned up, hunh?"

"You should talk to Victor, is what you should do."

That idea slid down my back like a pitcher of ice water. "Emma, I can't!"

"You have to!"

"I'm scared!"

"Well, sure. But it won't be as bad as you think." She took off her glasses, which had gotten smeared with tears, and wiped them off on her shirt. "And you owe him that much."

"*Arg!* Why do you have to be right all the time!"

Emma put her glasses back on. "It is my curse."

We started walking back up toward the museum. "You really are the smartest, bravest, most loyal person I know," I said. "I don't deserve to have a friend like you."

"Do you . . . do you really think so?" Emma asked, barely audible.

"I do."

"In that case," she said, giving me a watery smile, "when I call you up, **answer your bloody phone.**" And then she whacked me on the side of the head. Pretty hard, actually, but I deserved it.

Cathy's Ring

I was still trying to work up the courage to go find Victor when the front doors of the museum swung open, and he came out with Denny, helping Jewel down to the front curb where a taxi was pulling up. Denny and Jewel got into the cab; Victor turned and headed slowly back up the steps to where Emma and I were standing.

"Whoops," Emma said. "I think this is my cue to go."

I grabbed her arm. "Don't!"

She pried my fingers up one by one. "Cathy, don't be a baby. It will be fine."

I felt my mouth go dry and my knees get shaky as Victor got closer. "Do you promise?"

"Not in any contractually binding way." Emma removed my claw from her around her arm and backed away. "Hey there, Victor!" she called down the steps. "Cathy was just saying how much she wanted to talk to you!"

"You are the worst, most disloyal friend in the world," I hissed, "and I will personally—Oh, hey, Victor! Thanks for helping Jewel, there." He gave a

wan smile as Emma, the snake, slithered off leaving me to my doom. "So," I said. "Where are Denny and Jewel going?"

"SF General."

I wondered if Paper Folding Man would still be there in the emergency waiting room, sitting like a man on a riverbank, watching mortal lives rush and swirl in front of him, like so many leaves borne on a stream and carried finally down to the sea.

"Jewel will be okay. Two or three broken ribs, I think."

I nodded. "So . . . will she ever play the accordion again?"

Victor grinned. "It's a long road, a lot of rehab, but yeah, I think she will live to polka once more." His smile faded. "Actually, I was about to go look for you. I have something for you. Two things, actually."

"Do either of them involve bear traps, or electroshock, or pepper spray?" I said. "Because if they did, I would understand."

He grinned. "No pepper spray." He cautiously lowered himself to the steps and let out a long breath. "Mortality sucks."

147.

"Headache?"

"And dizzy. And just kind of generally confused. I assume it's the concussion, although being around you tends to have that effect on me anyway."

I sat down next to him, but not so close that we were touching. How easily I had come to take leaning against him for granted. Now the six inches between us felt like a million miles. "You're being very nice to me," I said quietly.

"Were you expecting something else? I love you—or had you forgotten?"

I looked at him blankly. "Oh," I said. "You don't know. They didn't tell you."

"About the hotel? Denny told me."

"He told you? He told you everything? We kissed," I said, "and—"

Victor laid a finger over my sad red clown mouth. "Shh. Yes, he told me everything."

"Then . . . I don't understand," I said humbly. "You gave up everything for me. You gave your life for me. And I—" I thought I had cried myself dry with Emma, but my stupid eyes filled up and overflowed again, sending two

little streams sliding down my improvised whiteface.

"Shhh. Easy there." Victor pulled a handful of bright yellow napkins out of his pocket, liberated from Little Sister's party supplies. "Here's one of the things I brought for you," he murmured. Gently he started wiping the makeup off my cheeks. "Judging by what it took to get Jewel cleaned up, we might be here a while. Mind you, crying helps. Good solvent," he said, showing me the napkin covered with white gloop.

"Yes, tears: well-known mascara remover." I hiccupped a little laugh. It didn't stop me from crying at all.

Victor wiped gently around my eyes, taking off white base makeup and the green and blue swirls I had used for decoration on top of it. "The first thing to remember is that you were tired and you were scared. You didn't know if any of us would even live to see the next day."

"But—"

"Second, I have never owned you," Victor said. "And I never will. Taking the serum doesn't change that."

Maybe it was all the hours without sleep, but my skin seemed supernaturally sensitive to the napkin as he rubbed it across my forehead and around my temples and along the line of my jaw. "But—"

"Third, you're eighteen years old, Cathy. I'm not. I know that sounds condescending, and that's not how I feel at all." Wiping around to the back of my neck and then a long slow caress along my throat. "I've been through this before, remember? I've fallen in love and fallen out of it," he said. "Married, divorced, been full of jealous rage. . . . Been the cause of it, for that matter." He took out another napkin and started to wipe off my sad red mouth. "Do I like the idea of you snuggling with some other guy? No. I hate it. A lot. But I'm also a grown-up. If in any way you still want to be with me, I wouldn't let something as small as twenty minutes in a hotel wreck the love of my life, not in a thousand years." He cracked a smile. "And since I don't have a thousand years left any more, I sure as hell don't want to screw up the next sixty."

The napkin passed under my mouth, beside it, his fingers touching my lips through the paper. I had stopped crying, but my face was flushed and hot and it was hard to breathe. "You're giving me another chance?"

He put the napkin down and pulled a small box out of his pocket. "I said I had two things for you. This is the other one." He opened the box and I saw a ring inside. "It's not expensive," he said quickly. "It's not a wedding ring. Honestly, you're eighteen. You don't need to be getting married yet, even to me." He took the ring out of the box. It was a simple band engraved with two symbols, a heart and an infinity sign. "Consider this a . . . placeholder. A promissory note. If, after a few years, you want to replace it with something fancier . . ." Victor met my eyes. "Something gold, for instance . . . you just let me know." He picked up my right hand and slid the ring onto my finger. "Your time, Cathy. Your choice."

I reached over and grabbed his shirt and leaned so close I bumped into his face with my antenna ball nose. "I think you should kiss me," I said huskily, and he did.

*

Time began.

The End.

Is that girl smart or what!!!

Phone numbers disconnected

Send Now | Print ▾ | Insert ▾ | Categories ▾ | Projects ▾

To: private@cathyskey.com
Cc:

Subject: Phone numbers disconnected
▶ Attachments: *none*

Verdana ▾ 14 ▾ **B** *I* U T

Hey Cathy–

Just doing a routine check, I noticed Bianca had disconnected her number and it looks like some messages have been deleted, too.

Can you test the archive? Go to www.doubletalkwireless.com

"Check Messages"

Try putting in Bianca's number: 510-286-7995. You should hear her answering machine message.

Then, if you put in her password (1111), you can hear the message Victor left for her.

(The password is her birthday, BTW – November 11. Remember V mumbled something about it being a special day?)

Your personal bug Tester,

E

Carla's Home # is on the daytimer page in Cathy's Book! (access code 1493)

Carla's Office: 408-236-3715

Just listened to message on Emma's phone at code 3030 whoa!!!

Victor... erased message at access code 5555 (where'd that come from?)